BOOK 8 OF MORNA'S LEGACY SERIES

LOVE BEYOND REACH

A SCOTTISH TIME TRAVEL ROMANCE

BETHANY CLAIRE

Editor: Dj Hendrickson
Cover Designer: Damonza

Available In eBook & Paperback

eBook ISBN: 978-0-9961136-5-6
Paperback ISBN: 978-0-9961136-6-3

http://www.bethanyclaire.com

For my readers,
You guys have tremendous patience.
Thank you so much.

Prologue

"So…what do ye think?" The question tumbled nervously from my lips. He'd taken his time reading our story. Each passing hour might as well have been a day as slowly as the minutes seemed to pass.

Spells, matchmaking, meddling—these were my talents, not writing—but my need to get our story down into a tangible form was so great that it had nearly driven me mad. My hands ached from the hours, days, and months spent working on my great project. Now that it was in front of my husband being read for the first time, I was sick with nerves.

"Did ye exaggerate for creative purposes?"

I knew without looking at the pages, without asking him, just what details in my story he questioned. I wouldn't lie to him to spare his feelings—not after so many years together. Our secrets were ours to keep but there was no room for lies between us.

"No."

"Hmm." He nodded in unison with the small noise. He may have wished for me to say otherwise, but he expected the answer I gave him. "I never knew ye loved him. I thought…"

My husband shook his head as he reached for me. Both our hands were wrinkled and weathered from time, but the feel of his touch still quickened my pulse in a way little else could. Time was powerless in dampening my desire for him.

"I thought ye stayed there to wait for me to return to ye, not because ye were happy at his side. But ye were. No matter how glad ye were to have me back, it broke yer heart to leave him. I dinna see that then. I am sorry for it. I am sorry for anything that has ever caused ye pain, but by God, I am glad that ye chose me."

"All hearts must be broken now and then." I smiled and squeezed his hand. "And I was there waiting for ye. 'Tis only that I often wondered if my waiting would do any good. But ye have to know that there was never any choice for me to make. It was always ye."

I wasn't sure my words would ease the pain I knew he must feel after reading certain parts of my story, but every word I said to him was true.

"Morna, who is this story meant for? I know that 'tis not only for us."

My husband knew me too well. Our story was meant especially for another—to lead her to the man worthy of holding her heart.

"There is a lass—the next to go back—that I intend to share my writing with. There are lessons she can learn from our story—lessons she will need before she makes a great journey of her own."

"Hmm."

My eyes were still turned toward our joined hands but I glanced up in response to his soft noise.

"What? Say whatever it is ye mean to. I canna stand it when ye beat around things so."

"Ye keep saying that 'tis our story, but 'tis not yet that. What ye have written here…'tis yer story."

He was right. It was the story of how we came to be, of all the events that led up to our life together, but there are two sides to every story, and I truly only knew my own.

"Aye, but I doona know what ye wish me to do about it. The only way for me to know all that happened in yer own life during that time is for me to spell ye, and I promised ye long ago that I wouldna do that. Unless ye finally mean to tell me everything."

Through our years together, he'd shared bits and pieces, but I never saw reason to press him on the subject. As long as we were together, I was fine with letting the past stay there. After all, I had plenty of my own secrets that I'd kept hidden until now.

"I willna tell ye a thing, but perhaps I shall try writing down my version just as ye have done. If 'tis rubbish when I finish, ye doona have to include it with what ye leave for the lass. Will ye let me try?"

Of course I would. Despite his modesty, he knew full well that whatever he wrote down wouldn't be rubbish. My husband was a closeted creative—I had a chest full of love letters and poems to prove it.

"Aye. Can ye finish it within three weeks? The lass arrives then."

He stood, still clinging to the pages he held in his hand and winked at me as he moved toward the stairs.

"I'll have it finished in half that time. The words are surfacing even now."

Conall Castle—Three Weeks Later

I t was odd for me to be watched so closely in the place that had once been my childhood home. I stood nervously inside the familiar walls of my old bedchamber, twisting my head at every noise or possible footstep to make certain no other tourists or castle employees were headed in our direction.

"It sure looks good, Morna. You did a really good job of making the outside look like a bunch of the other old books here. Do you have another copy? I want to read it."

A brief moment of terror filled me at the thought of Cooper opening the pages of my book and taking in the words inside. He understood far too much about everything already. The last thing he ever needed to read was every little—and sometimes scandalous—detail of my life.

"Cooper, if ye love me, ye will promise me to never, ever read what I've written. It is meant for someone else's eyes, and those are not yer own. Do ye understand?"

While young Coop usually did the exact opposite of what he was told, I could see by the concerned look in his eyes that he cared enough about my plea to listen this time.

"Fine, but I know what that means. It means there's the same stuff in this book as in the books that Mom used to read when we lived in New York. I bet you talk about kissing in there, huh?"

I could live with it if all Cooper thought was inside those pages was a little kissing. "Aye, Cooper. I'll admit there is some mention of kissing within that wee book."

"Yuck." Cooper's expression twisted into one of disgust, and he held the book away from him as if he worried the nearness of it might allow him to absorb the words. "You don't need to say anything else. I promise to never read it. But can I ask you one more thing? Why did you want me to come?"

I laughed but didn't argue the point with him. I had, in fact, not wanted him to come. If not for Cooper's unexpected arrival at our home a week ago, I would've brought the book to the castle myself but, as was customary for Cooper, he'd been quite insistent on coming with me. Apparently, now that I'd given him a job to do, he felt needed enough to forget the previous conversation.

"I suppose I just thought that mischief is more fun in the company of others, and I know how good ye are at keeping a secret. I can trust ye to keep a secret, aye? Ye know how the others feel about my meddling. I doona wish to explain it all to them."

If Cooper felt he had an important role to play in anything, he was sure to meet it head-on.

"Of course you can. Don't you worry. How long do you think it will take for her to find it up here?"

I couldn't be certain. I would no longer spell anyone to do exactly as I wished them to, but I would always point people in the direction I knew they needed to go.

"I hope not verra long at all. She's here actually. In the castle at this verra moment."

5

"Really?" Cooper's voice rose several octaves in his excitement. "Can you show her to me on our way out? I promise I won't say anything to her. Let's just walk by her or something, okay?"

I was just as keen to see the woman in person myself. "Aye, fine. Now, hurry before someone finds us." I paused and pointed in the direction of the small table next to a sitting chair in the corner of the room. "Ye see there? Lay it just there as quickly as ye can. Then we must be on our way. Magic works best if ye set it and then release it to do as it should."

"Aye, aye, Morna. I am your humble servant, Pirate Cooper."

"A pirate? Have ye moved on from dinosaurs then?"

Cooper's voice, when he answered, sounded astonished and horrified.

"Move on from dinosaurs? Are you crazy? I don't think I could ever do that. But a man has to have varied interests. It makes him well-rounded."

I laughed at him and gently reached for his shoulder to steer him from the room.

"Right ye are, Cooper. Ye are a well-rounded young man, indeed."

It was my every memory—my husband's, as well—and I hoped that when the lass found it, she would treasure every word. Only time would tell.

"**I** think this one is my favorite, so far. There's just a feeling to it. I don't know what it is, really. Something magical about it, wouldn't you say?"

Laurel turned and awaited Marcus' response. She could tell by his glazed expression that her usually patient friend was losing his resolve to indulge her obsession with all things old.

"You've said that about every castle. Each one is more magical than the last, each new one is now your favorite. I'll be honest, they are all starting to look the same to me—just one big blur of stones and crumbling junk."

While many sites they'd visited over the last ten days had indeed been crumbling, Conall Castle in no way fit that description. Well-tended and magnificent, Laurel could all but see the castle's history swirling around her—could almost feel the people who lived here before.

"That's because they do keep getting more magical. I swear it. Especially this one. But you know, it may just feel that way because it seems like we are the only ones here. It's lovely to have the whole castle to ourselves rather than bumping into other tourists around every corner."

Marcus laughed and Laurel knew what he was going to say before he uttered a word. He'd complained about it for the entirety of the drive.

"It doesn't surprise me that we are the only ones here. I know lots of the places we've visited have been isolated, but this is quite literally in the middle of nowhere. If our car broke down on the way back tonight, there would be nowhere for us to stay."

Laurel found herself hoping, however wrong, that the car would break down just before dusk. She couldn't think of anything more enjoyable than being stranded amid such beauty.

"I don't think I would care too much if we got stuck out here. Surely a castle as old as this wouldn't be too hard to slip into after everyone leaves for the night. To sleep in a place like this would be pure heaven."

Marcus couldn't sound less enthused. "It probably has ghosts."

"Oh, I hope so. All of the best ones do."

Marcus' hand on her forearm drew her attention away from the tall window she stood gazing out of. "Hey, look. We're not alone, after all. Still, I agree with you that it's nice being around fewer people."

Sure enough, as Laurel turned she could see two people approaching—an older woman accompanied by a young boy who held himself very proudly as he walked.

"Let's head down toward the other end, Marcus, so that they have this area of the castle to themselves."

The woman and boy said nothing to either of them as they passed, but Laurel found herself struck by the intensity of the unabashed stare she received from both of them. She gave them a friendly smile in return, and the young boy raised his left hand and waved in greeting before they went on their way.

"Did you see the way they both stared at me? Has my blouse popped open or something?"

Laurel looked self-consciously down at herself as she tried to make sense of their wide, questioning eyes.

"No. Everything is covered as far as I can tell. Maybe they recognized you."

Laurel laughed and continued to move down the long hallway toward the last room at its end.

"Did you see how small that child was? There is no way he knows who I am. If his parents let him read one of my books at his age, then God help him. No, it definitely wasn't that. Maybe they were staring at you, and I just mistook the direction of the boy's gaze."

"Because I'm black? Come on, Laurel. Surely you think better of them than that."

Laurel couldn't tell if he was joking, but it wouldn't surprise her if he wasn't. Marcus had so many wonderful qualities. While his humility was to be admired, it drove her crazy just how incapable he seemed of recognizing his own attractiveness.

"No, Marcus. I most definitely didn't think they were staring at you because you are black. Perhaps they were staring at you because the only other human I've seen with your shape is the guy who plays Captain America."

Marcus huffed and stepped into the room to their right.

"I can already predict what you are going to say about this room."

Laurel remained just outside the doorway as she awaited his prediction.

"Oh yeah? What's that?"

"You are going to say that out of all the castles and all the rooms you've seen, this is by far your favorite."

She knew he teased her. Regardless, he was bound to be wrong. The room that lay ahead of her couldn't possibly beat the tower room they'd seen in the castle two days before.

"Let's just see about that, shall we?"

Determined to come up with a reaction opposite of what Marcus expected, Laurel stepped inside, looked around, and found herself completely unable to do so.

The room was perfect in every way. The things she loved most in all the world lined three of the four walls—books.

"It drives me crazy when you're right. This beats the tower."

"I knew you were going to say that. I knew it even before I stepped inside. I read about it in the guidebook and knew you'd love it. I can see by the happy, glazed expression on your face that you'll be in here a while. I think I'll go explore the dungeon while you do so. I'll come back for you in a bit."

Marcus nudged her playfully before leaving her alone in the room. Once he was gone, she inhaled deeply and smiled. The smell of books gave her the same kind of energy coffee did for some. She thrived off them, lived in them, made her living from them. In a room full of books, she felt at home.

She knew that the books lining the shelves didn't quite fit the historical nature of the castle—the bindings and covers were enough to tell her that none could be more than a hundred years old. Still, that knowledge did not reduce her love for what surrounded her now.

She moved to the far wall and slowly trailed her fingers along the spines moving row after row, bottom to top. It was a game she often played in libraries—letting her fingers trail the spines of many books until she felt something draw her to one in particular. As her fingers moved, she glanced to her left and took notice of a lone book sitting on a side table. Her fingers moved toward it instinctively.

10

She only resisted sitting on the old piece of furniture for a few seconds. As she picked up the book, she sank into the soft, empty chair, eager to read.

The chair was old and for a moment she feared it would collapse underneath her, but as she settled in more fully, it seemed to wrap her up in a way that invited her to do nothing more than read.

Marcus would occupy himself for ages while exploring the castle grounds. It wouldn't hurt anyone for her to take a moment to herself.

She opened the book gently. While it surprised her to see that the words were in English, it was the handwritten note inside that piqued her interest in a way nothing else ever had.

> *To whomever finds this book, you should know that it was meant just for you. Tuck it away in your bag, hide it beneath your shirt, but whatever you do, do not return it to the place it rested before. For many would read the pages contained within and dismiss my every memory and word as nothing more than fiction. But you, my first and last reader, will read these words and hear the truth in them.*
>
> *Read these words. Love them, tend to them, believe them, and then once you've made peace with the truth, come and find me. By my story's end, you will know where.*
>
> *Until we meet,*
> *Morna Conall*

P.S. Those who know me well know I have a terrible habit of butting in pretty much whenever I feel like it, and I'm afraid I found myself doing the same thing with my writing. As I was preparing my story, I realized that in some instances my conversational voice—sort of like this letter—was needed to show you even more. These little intrusions are scattered throughout the book. Think of them as author notes, if you will.

P.P.S. My husband has also seen fit to throw in his two cents, so you'll find parts of the book written by him, as well. It may all sound rather confusing now, but I have a keen sense of just how bright you are. You'll have no trouble at all, I'm sure. Now, get to reading. We have no time to waste.

"**D**amn." Laurel whispered the word aloud to herself, shaking her head at the book with mesmerized awe. Whatever the reason for such strange words, the author must have known that it would be impossible for the reader who stumbled upon them to do anything other than read on. She didn't know anyone whose curiosity would allow them to do differently. Smiling at the wit and the wonder of it, Laurel happily flipped to the next page and continued reading, never suspecting for a moment how such an act would change her life forever.

Chapter 1

Note from M.C. (Morna Conall)

I told you these would be scattered throughout the book. Here's the first one—right at the beginning.

The summer of my twelfth year was one of the most tragic and difficult seasons of my life. Looking back, those dark days marked the end of my childhood in a way that forever changed the person I was destined to become. Had my grandmother lived longer, had Grier not been forced to leave, had my father not seen fit to upend my world by telling me a truth I never really needed to know, perhaps magic would've come more easily to me, perhaps I could've saved one of my dearest friends in the world, perhaps I would've been content to live out my days healing villagers rather than pushing my way into the love lives of nearly everyone I've ever known and loved.

Perhaps, perhaps, perhaps...those questions never really get us anywhere, do they?

Still, memories have a way of sneaking into our minds when we least expect them. Most especially—in my experience—when we don't want them to. If I could tell you my story without reliving those few dreadful July days so many years ago, I certainly would. After all, this is a story of a young woman, not that of a little girl.

But the effects of this time were too far-reaching for me to exclude them from my story. So for the briefest of moments, allow me to break your heart.

I promise everything will work out in the end.

Conall Castle—Summer of 1613

"What do ye mean, what do I want in a husband? I doona want a husband. Not ever."

I collapsed onto the thick blanket spread out on the ground for our lesson and looked up at Grier with confusion. Even though I was still terrible at magic, I looked forward to our daily lessons. It was the only time of day I felt like myself. While my progress was slow, my skills improved with each passing day. I saw no need to waste my precious learning time visiting about something so entirely useless.

Grier's smile didn't quite reach her eyes as she moved to sit across from me on the blanket. Her gaze looked haunted and suddenly older. For the briefest of moments, I wondered if perhaps the rumors about her were true. Maybe Grier really was much older than she appeared.

Despite the occasional weariness I sometimes saw in her eyes, Grier carried herself with an otherworldly confidence that enchanted all who knew her. I was fairly certain that everyone I'd ever known was at least halfway in love with Grier. Everyone that is, except my father. He detested my mentor. If not for Grandmother's insistence that she stay and teach me how to use my magic, he would've sent Grier away long ago.

It wasn't that Father didn't find her attractive. I knew that he did. Sometimes, I would catch him looking at her in the same way that Alasdair and every other male in the castle did. He simply hated that anyone might have more power than him. I suspected he hated me for the same reason.

"Grier...how old are ye?"

This time her smile was genuine, and my body released tension I hadn't even known it carried. That was Grier's power. In her presence, her mood quickly became your own.

"Do ye know how often I get asked that? How many times do ye imagine I've answered it?"

Grier almost always answered questions in this way. Never really answering anything, she could masterfully redirect a question.

"If it has to do with magic, ye should tell me, even if ye've never told anyone else before. Ye are the only other witch I've ever known. Ye are the only person I have to learn from."

Her eyes shifted again—back to the saddened, distant gaze of before.

"I'm verra old, though I'll never tell anyone just how old, for 'tis truly of no importance. My soul is still twenty and always shall be. Aging, or the lack thereof, is not what we are discussing today. All I will say is this, witches doona age in

15

the same way as everyone else. One day, ye will be able to decide just how old ye wish to appear, and ye will be able to keep yerself that way for as long as ye like."

Every day the new wonders of magic astonished me. How could I have been so fortunate to be blessed with it when no one else in my family had ever had magic before? My great fortune amazed me.

"No. Ye canna mean it. If 'tis true, why canna we discuss this today? I'd much rather learn about this than discuss my getting a husband."

Grier sighed and the exhaustion in it washed over me, making my limbs heavy and tired.

"Ye needn't worry about getting a husband right now. Ye are only twelve. Even though many are wed at yer age, yer own father—bastard that he is—wouldna marry ye off so young. When ye are wed, he can no longer control ye, and he derives too much pleasure from that to rid himself of ye so soon. I only mean to make certain that the man ye do marry is the man ye wish to."

I smiled in awe. Everyone shared her sentiment about my father, but none save her would ever dare say so. She was the most fearless person I'd ever known.

"If I am not to be married, why should we concern ourselves with this now?"

"I'll tell ye after we cast the spell. We've not much time. This is far too important to leave unattended. Now, while I believe that ye doona want a husband now, someday ye shall want someone with whom to share yer life. I've already seen the sort of man yer father would choose for ye, and I willna stand for it. Sit quietly and close yer eyes."

16

Begrudgingly, I did as she asked.

"What am I meant to be thinking?"

"Shhh."

Grier laughed softly as she silenced me. I could sense her moving closer. While my eyes remained closed, she took my hands. Slowly, she turned them over and began to trace patterns on the soft flesh of my palms with her pointer fingers.

"Ye doona need to think a thing. 'Twill be easier for me to see what ye will need if ye quiet yer mind."

For a long while, Grier said nothing. Eventually, ever so slowly, my thoughts began to settle as I was lulled into a quiet, peaceful trance by Grier's soft touch.

When she spoke, her voice was soft and smooth. My entire body warmed through. I felt as if I could float away. I was as calm, safe, and happy as I'd ever been in my life.

"Look how lovely ye will be. I wouldna have thought it possible for yer hair to grow any thicker. Do ye feel that stubborn fire rising inside ye? Ach, I'm glad to see that it remains after what is coming for ye soon."

Something at the edge of my mind prickled uncomfortably at Grier's warning, but I was too comfortable underneath Grier's spell to pay it any mind.

"As I feared, yer father will do everything in his power to discourage yer power. Ye will need someone who encourages ye, who is not afraid of him, who gives ye a purpose to move forward."

In my mind, I stood in front of mirrored glass, but my reflection was different. I was older, more womanly in shape, and my face was less soft and childlike. I smiled and was secretly pleased to see that my teeth hadn't twisted as I'd grown.

"Morna, each of us with magic has our own special set of gifts. Mine is to teach. A rather boring gift in the realm of what we do. Ye possess a gift that is far more interesting and, indeed, far more rare. It is within yer skill set that I've found the man who can help ye."

I wanted to call out and ask her what she meant, what my skill set was, but I couldn't move from the place inside my mind. My voice remained silent.

"I've never done it before, but I believe I can. I'll simply pull from the untapped power within ye. Allow me to stay here just a few moments more. I need to get a clear picture. I need to find him in time."

The image in the mirror swirled. Slowly my reflection was replaced with that of a man. Broad-shouldered and tan, he didn't resemble any of the men I knew. While most wore their hair long, his was cut to just below his ears though the hair on top hung long and wavy. He had no beard, but stubble lined his jaw. His eyes were kind.

The intensity of his gaze caused my breath to catch. I tried to look away, intimidated by his stare, uncomfortable with the feeling of intimacy that built between us. I couldn't move. My eyes remained locked with the stranger's as Grier spoke.

"Aye...'tis not yet time for him to come, but in a few years ye will be ready for him. A few minutes more and the spell will be complete."

I didn't want this man in my life. I could feel the chaos that his presence would bring, and it frightened me more than anything in my life ever had. I wanted to scream to stop her, but nothing would come.

Instead, everything went black as pain ripped at me from the top of my head down to the tips of my toes. I tried to breathe. When no air entered my lungs, the darkness spun.

I lost all consciousness as I faded into the nothingness that surrounded me.

I woke three days later, exhausted, confused, and totally unprepared for the hellish world that awaited me. Alasdair knelt beside my bed, both of his hands gripping mine tightly as he sobbed next to my bed.

"Morna, I'm sorry. I'm so, so sorry. Please wake up. I canna do this without ye."

He repeated the words over and over. The dread in his voice pulled me from my deep slumber too quickly. My head ached horribly, and I could only vaguely remember where I'd been before.

The meadow. My lesson. Slowly, memory came back to me. I sat up and pulled my hands from Alasdair's grip.

"The spell...what happened? Where's Grier?"

His face was red, his eyes swollen from crying. Fear lodged itself deep in my chest. In that instant, I wanted nothing more than to be sleeping again, to lose myself in the darkness of my dreamless sleep.

"She...she's gone."

19

My brother was a grown man sixteen years my senior, yet he looked so young and broken that terror gripped me so tightly I trembled as I struggled to speak.

"How long have I been asleep? What do ye mean she's gone?"

He rose from the floor and sat at the end of my bed, composing himself as best he could.

"Ye've been asleep for three days. I was so frightened that ye wouldna ever wake. I doona know what Grier was doing to ye, but it dinna go as she planned. Father interrupted ye both. I followed after him but I couldna stop him.

"When I reached him in the field where ye have yer lessons, Grier was standing over ye, muttering words neither of us could understand. She was pulling something from ye—a bright light poured from yer chest and ye were lifting off the ground. Grier was so lost in her spell that she dinna hear Father approach. Had she seen him, I canna imagine what she would've done to him."

He shook his head and paused, struggling for composure. In his silence, I frantically sorted through my memories of that day, searching for any recollection of what Alasdair described. I found nothing. I could remember a mirror and the hazy image of a man standing before me. Then there was only darkness.

"What did he do to her?"

"He pushed her to the ground, breaking her spell. Ye fell. Then he pulled ye up and threw ye over his horse. Ye wouldna wake. Grier screamed at him over and over, telling him to put ye down. She said that if she dinna finish the spell, 'twould damage ye, but Da dinna care. He said if it damaged ye enough to rid ye of magic, ye'd be better off for it.

"He banished Grier. Dinna even allow her to take her things. He told her that if she dinna leave his land right away, he would have her burned for witchcraft."

I swallowed. My mouth was so dry I could scarcely speak, but I couldn't allow him to continue to tell me something I knew couldn't be true. Grandmother would never allow Father to send Grier away.

"She canna be gone for long though, aye? Grandmother will see her back to the castle."

I saw it then, the deep well of grief in Alasdair's eyes. Before he could say a word, I knew what he'd been trying to tell me all along. Of course Grandmother would never allow Father to behave in such a way. If Grier was gone, Grandmother was too.

He opened his arms to me as I collapsed against him, my sobs lodging in my chest as I struggled to breathe against the shock.

"She passed in her sleep. That was why Father went to the field—to tell ye. He's been lost in his drink ever since. I havena left yer side, Morna. I've been so worried for ye. If ye'd died as well, I would've killed him. I know I would have."

I don't remember how long he held me. I eventually fell asleep again, drained from a grief so deep that I feared I would never recover. When next I woke, I found the dark, angry, bloodshot eyes of my father staring down at me.

"Rise. Ye have spent too long abed."

I couldn't move. Every time I opened my eyes, a fresh wave of grief hit me.

I said nothing. I simply couldn't bring myself to care that my inaction would anger him. My heart was too broken to feel anything other than loss.

"Do ye think ye are the only one devastated by this loss, Morna? Everyone in this castle is hurting. We must all carry on."

"I only learned of her death today. Did the rest of ye carry on the day it happened? Are ye so cruel as to not allow me even a day to grieve the loss of my grandmother?"

Father's voice was cold and slurred. He never drank, but on this night, he was so deep in his cups he could barely stand.

"Ha. 'Tis ye that's cruel. 'Tis not kind of ye to make me worry about how upset ye are over my mother's death. She is not yers to grieve over."

Between sobs, I screamed at him.

"How can ye say that? She was the only mother I've ever known."

"She was not yer mother. Nor was she yer grandmother."

For a moment, I wasn't sure I heard him correctly. He turned to leave my room, but strength I didn't know I possessed lifted me from the bed as I hurried to block him.

"What did ye say?"

Tears filled his eyes, and I gasped as he pulled me against him in a tight embrace. Father never hugged me. His breath ragged, he rested his chin on the top of my head as he spoke.

"Surely, ye've suspected it. I know ye believe I hate ye. I doona. I hate yer mother. Her dying act was to leave me with a

22

child that dinna belong to me. Now, dress and join the rest of us for dinner. We willna wait for ye."

He pushed me away and left. As the door to my bedchamber closed, I sank to the floor and lost myself in heartbreaking sobs.

Only three days before, my world had been bright and full of hope. Now, all I could see was loss. Two of the people I loved most were gone without a goodbye, and despite my complicated feelings about my father, I'd never once suspected what he'd revealed.

Alasdair was now the only person I had left in all the world.

My childhood was over.

Chapter 2

Eight Years Later —1620

Much changed at Conall Castle following my grandmother's death. At our father's insistence, no one within or around the castle ever spoke of Grier again. Within a fortnight of her banishment, all evidence of her time with us was gone. Already heartbroken and grieving over the loss of our grandmother, Alasdair and I were forced to wade through the deep loss of our friend alone.

My magic practices ceased entirely—or at least that's what Alasdair and I worked day and night to lead our father to believe. I continued to practice as much as I could, but with no one to guide me, I made little progress. My apparent lack of magic pleased my father immensely and as I grew, his treatment of me improved. My feelings toward him remained unchanged. How much can you love someone who only loves the version of you that they want you to be?

I didn't hate my father—I pitied his incurable unhappiness—but I couldn't bring myself to love him, at least not in the way I loved my brother and friends.

Despite his confession that he wasn't actually my father, I never allowed myself to travel down the uncertain path of wallowing in that revelation. Even if what he claimed was true, it mattered little. Simply by claiming me as his own, I'd been afforded a life that most people in Scotland would only ever dream of. Even as miserable and mean as he was, I had to be grateful to him for that.

Three years after that terrible summer, Alasdair fell in love and married one of the most beautiful women I'd ever seen— Elspeth—a shy but strong woman who stole his heart the moment he laid eyes on her. At the age of thirty-one, most in Conall territory had begun to believe that Alasdair would never marry, so his nuptials with Elspeth were met with wondrous celebrations that lasted nearly a month.

Two years later, they welcomed a beautiful baby boy, Eoin, making me the happiest aunt that ever lived. Before the child's birth, I spent years roaming around the castle with no real purpose. Now three, Eoin had grown into an energetic and abnormally-tall-for-his-age child that spent every spare moment following me around. As a result, I was the closest thing that wee Eoin ever had to a nurse, and I loved every moment of it. My father, Elspeth, and even Alasdair—who usually tolerated everything I did—hated it. Childcare was a servant's work, and they all believed my role in Eoin's rearing was below my station as daughter of the laird.

It wasn't only them. Everyone I knew seemed to be deeply worried about me in one way or another.

Nearing twenty, the villagers seemed to have the same fears about me now that they'd had for Alasdair. I was quickly reaching an age where few would wish to marry me, and I knew my father well enough to know that he wouldn't let such a problem go unresolved for long. My days of freedom were bound to end soon. Until they did, I was determined to enjoy every moment with those I knew and loved. Thoughts of true adulthood could come later.

"Again, again."

I squeezed my nephew tight and grinned as his long legs bounced up and down against my thighs as he squirmed in my lap. Eoin pointed to the candles, urging me with his limited vocabulary to blow them out and relight them with my magic. For at least the eighth time that night, I flicked my wrist and watched the room go dark.

Bending in close to his ear, I whispered, "Only once more. Then ye must go to bed. Do ye avoid sleep in this manner when yer mother tucks ye in?"

Eoin simply laughed and continued to point to the candles as I re-lit the room. It was one of the few spells I could work without worry of something going dreadfully wrong, but even this must end soon. Eoin's speech improved quickly. I would have to stop doing magic in front of him before he mentioned the candles to my father.

With the room now lit, I stood and carried Eoin to his bed, tucking him gently inside. He yawned as I wrapped the blankets around him. I knew it wouldn't take long for him to fall asleep.

Most nights his mother saw him to bed, but Elspeth had appeared so weary at dinner that I insisted she go to bed early. With my brother away for the next month, I imagined that she was due a few weeks of uncrowded, peaceful sleep.

Just as Eoin began to drift, he suddenly jolted awake and reached beneath the covers for something he'd bumped against with his foot.

I watched as he pulled a large book from beneath the blanket. I took it curiously as he extended it to me.

27

I knew he couldn't read. Neither could Elspeth. Had Alasdair begun to read to him at night?

"Is this yer da's?"

Eoin shook his head and squirmed back until he sat up in the bed.

"No. I found it."

I held the book, flipped it over in my hands, and looked suspiciously down at him.

"Ye found it? Where did ye find it?"

Books were rarely left just lying around the castle. As far as I knew, only Father, Alasdair, and myself could read.

Eoin scooted out from beneath the blanket and crawled to the end of the bed until he could look all the way down the hallway to his right. Slowly, he lifted his finger and pointed to the room at the very end—my father's bedchamber.

I lowered my head and lifted my brows as I looked up at him questioningly.

"Ye found it or ye took it?"

The young child just smiled and returned to snuggle in beneath his blankets.

"Ye can bring it back. I doona want it."

Why the child wanted it in the first place, I couldn't guess. For the first time, I opened the book to its middle and looked inside.

A deep chill swept down the length of my body as I flipped hurriedly through the pages.

Spells in Grier's hand filled the book's entirety.

For eight long years my magic remained stagnant while assistance unknowingly lay only a hall's length away—hidden by my close-minded, controlling father.

Trembling, I tapped the book's cover as I spoke.

"Did ye see other books like this? When did ye take it?"

He nodded, and his eyelids grew heavy as he started to drift into sleep.

"Aye, in a chest. I found it this morning when I hid from ye."

His little eyes closed. I sat perfectly still until his breathing deepened enough that I knew my leaving wouldn't wake him.

Grier's spell books were still in the castle. Soon they would be mine.

I would stop at nothing to learn to harness the magic that hummed with life inside of me.

Chapter 3

An entire week passed. With each new day, I grew more frustrated at my various failed attempts to steal Grier's books away from my father. Each time I believed him far enough away from his bedchamber to risk entry, I would find him in some unexpected part of the castle. It seemed that the more I wanted access to the books, the more difficult it became to evade my father's watchful eyes.

With Alasdair still away on a secret errand for our father, I was forced to wait until the perfect opportunity presented itself. Patience came to me as naturally as obedience did—I was rubbish at both. Still, there was no one else I would put in such danger. So wait I did.

The worst Alasdair or I would receive for sneaking into Father's bedchamber was a good tongue lashing. If a servant was caught rummaging through Father's things, the most lenient punishment they would receive was banishment.

Frustrated from days of thinking up entirely useless ideas, I went in search of Mary. Two years younger than me, she'd been with our family so long that at the age of only seventeen she ran our home with a level of authority surpassed only by my father. She was my dearest friend and the only person, save Alasdair, that encouraged my magic.

I found Mary just as I expected to—in our cold and damp basement kitchen, covered in flour, ordering around half a dozen girls between the ages of twelve and fifteen with a tone that made me pity each and every one of them.

The moment she saw me standing in the doorway, she wiped her hands on the bottom of her dress and turned to address one of the youngest girls in Gaelic before joining me in the doorway.

"I doona know why I bother trying to teach them. 'Twould be less work if I sent them all away and did everything myself."

As several of the young girls looked nervously in our direction, I pulled Mary away and lowered my voice as I answered her.

"Ye teach them for ye know their families need what little they earn here. Ye care more than ye like to show."

Ignoring me, Mary quickened her steps and motioned for me to follow.

"Come with me to the village. I promised Mae I would tend the inn this evening so she may care for her father. Ye can help me. He is verra unwell. I doona believe he will live past the end of the year."

"Ach, no." It would break Mae's heart to lose her father. She knew little of life outside caring for him. "Do ye truly think he willna recover this time?"

"Every breath is a struggle. I canna see how he could improve. Mae's accepted whatever will come. The lass is stronger than I hope I ever have to be."

"What will it take for yer brother to see that Mae is in love with him? She will need someone when her father passes, and they couldna be more perfectly suited."

32

Turning with the speed of someone half her size, Mary spun to face me and burst out laughing. Between strangled breaths, she spoke.

"Mae...Mae doesna love Hew. What possibly led ye to believe that?"

I found the intensity of the attraction between the two of them so obvious, it was difficult for me to imagine how Mary couldn't see it.

"'Tis clear to me every time I see the two of them together, and she is not the only one who carries such feelings. Hew cares for Mae so much he can scarcely keep from trembling in front of her."

Mary laughed even more loudly as we continued the short walk to the village just beyond the castle grounds.

"'Tis true that Hew is shy, but he wouldna tremble in front of anyone, most especially Mae. Why, he's known her his whole life. Mayhap, the unused magic within ye is poisoning yer mind. Ye've never been so wrong about anything in yer life."

Unaffected by her doubt, I glanced over at the castle stables as we passed. An idea popped into my mind. If Mary had so little faith in my ability to see what was right in front of me, I would make her believe by revealing a truth about herself I knew she'd never told another before.

"Are ye so certain that I'm wrong that ye'd wager against it?"

Mary's confidence often got her into trouble. I knew she wouldn't say no.

"O'course, I am. What do ye have in mind?"

"We shall ask Mae if she cares for Hew as I believe she does when we arrive at her inn. If she either flushes blood red or

33

says 'aye,' we will know that I am right. If I am right, which I am, ye must go and confess yer own feelings to the lad ye fancy most."

Laughing again, Mary stopped walking and doubled over as she gripped her stomach.

"Morna, ye must cease this. I havena laughed so much in weeks. I shall ache all day from it. Aye, I shall take yer wager for I canna lose."

Keeping my voice level, I smiled at Mary as she straightened.

"Lose ye will."

She shook her head and placed both her hands on her hips in defiance.

"But I canna lose, for ye know as well as I do that Mae doesna love my brother. Even if she does, I doona fancy any man around here. Thank God for it, too, for ye know how unseemly 'twould be for a woman to confess her feelings to someone she is not betrothed to."

Resuming her fast-paced trot toward the village, I ran to block her path.

"Mary, I know ye too well for ye to lie to me."

"I never lie."

"Aye, ye lie more than any good person ever should. Ye do care for a man here. Ye care for him verra much."

The amusement in her face faded, and I could see that she wondered just how I could possibly know.

"Oh? And who might that be?"

"Our stable master—Kip."

Even Mary's skin, darkened from too much time outdoors, flushed red at the mention of Kip's name. I beamed with triumph as I placed my hand on her shoulder.

"Did ye feel what yer face did? If Mae's does the same, we will know I was right."

Smiling, I turned and walked ahead of her.

My incessantly talkative friend fell silent.

Chapter 4

"Ye canna mean that ye truly intend to make me tell him. 'Twould be improper, and Kip wouldna care for it. 'Twill only make him uncomfortable. Please Morna, I beg ye. I'll do anything else."

Still in shock over losing the wager, Mary continued to protest as we made our way back to the castle in the dark. Upon arriving at Mae's inn, I sent word back to the castle to inform my father that Mae needed help and I would be absent from dinner, freeing Mary and me to tend to the inn until every last traveler was fed and abed for the night.

While father wouldn't approve of my helping in the inn any more than he did of my tending to Eoin, Mae's father and my own were old friends. I knew he would make no issue of my desire to help them if it was only for one night.

Of course I wouldn't force Mary to tell Kip of her feelings. I cared for my friend too much to embarrass her—not that I intended to tell her that just yet. Perhaps a few more minutes of dread would teach her to not doubt me so fiercely next time. While I wouldn't force Mary to say anything, I did intend to at least get Mary and Kip in the same room in the hopes that their feelings for one another might be strong enough to persuade one of them to take action.

"Aye, ye will tell him for I doona know if Kip will ever have the courage to do what he should without it. We will stop in at his cottage on the way to the castle."

Shaking her head in the moonlight, Mary repeated her astonishment for the tenth time since leaving the inn.

"I canna believe how easily Mae admitted it. She's never said a word about Hew before this night."

"'Tis no surprise to me that Mae answered ye honestly. Have ye ever known the lass to speak an untruth? I doona believe she's capable of it."

"Aye, I suppose 'tis true. Mae speaks her own mind too plainly to lie. Though, I must ask ye, Morna, did ye spell Mae to say what ye wished?"

An involuntary snort escaped me as I turned and looked at my friend to gauge the sincerity of her question.

"Mary, yer eye is still bruised from my attempt to send a wooden spoon across the kitchen to ye. Do ye truly believe I've the power to spell anyone to do anything?"

Rather than floating easily over to Mary's hand as intended, the spoon had flown across the kitchen with such speed that it smashed against her face and knocked her to the ground. She'd been angry with me for days.

Mary shrugged, keeping her voice low as she answered.

"I doona know what I believe about ye anymore. I still doona know how ye discerned my feelings for Kip. I've never even whispered them aloud to myself."

"'Tis a gift, not a spell. O'course I dinna spell Mae to do anything."

Kip's cottage lay just to the east of the castle's stables. His home was dark as we approached.

"Morna, he's already sleeping. We canna wake him up. I refuse to do it."

Pointing over to the stables, I grabbed her arm to prevent her from running off toward the castle.

"Look at the candlelight. He's still tending to the horses. I know he willna mind us visiting him there."

"Kip never works so late. If someone is within the stables, 'tis Rab, the newest stable hand."

Worry rolled off Mary in waves and her arm tensed beneath my grip. It was time to end her pain.

"Doona worry, Mary. I only mean to facilitate a meeting between the two of ye. Ye needn't say a thing that ye doona wish to as long as ye promise to not be so doubtful of me next time."

I smiled in the darkness as Mary sighed in relief.

"I'll never doubt ye again."

Inside, we found Kip leaning against the widest stall at the stable's far end staring intently at the mare inside. Hearing our approach, he turned to greet us. His smile was wide, and his eyes never left Mary. I wasn't even sure he knew I was there until he spoke.

"Did the two of ye come to see the birth?"

"Birth?" Mary's voice rose with excitement as she moved around me to look down into the stall.

I grinned inwardly as I slowly approached the two of them from behind. A birth would be the perfect excuse for Mary to linger. Perhaps she could offer him aid while I slipped away feigning exhaustion.

"Are ye alone, Kip? Shouldna Rab be here helping ye?"

Kip waved a dismissive hand and scooted near Mary so I could join them.

"Ach, the lad wouldna know what to do, and 'tis more trouble than 'tis worth to teach him. He said an errand—though he wouldna tell me what it was—needed his attention, and I saw no reason to keep him here."

Determined not to let this opportunity pass, I leaned forward to look across Kip at Mary.

"Kip, I canna believe our good fortune. Why, Mary was telling me only this morning that she'd never seen a mare give birth."

Eyes wide and disbelieving, Kip took over the conversation just as I'd hoped.

"No? Is this true, Mary? Surely, it canna be. Why, ye helped deliver Elspeth's baby all on yer own."

Blushing, Mary shot me a quick glance before answering him. I had no idea whether or not what I said was true, but I hoped she had enough sense to go along with it without question.

"Aye, 'tis true. Would ye mind if we stayed and watched? We'll help if we need to."

Yawning, I threw my arms above my head and stretched dramatically.

"Oh, Mary, I'm far too tired to stay, but I can see myself inside the castle if ye would like to wait for the birth."

In a gesture that surprised and filled me with hope, Kip reached out to gently touch Mary's arm as he spoke.

"Ye must stay. 'Tis a wondrous sight."

Content that my matchmaking would carry on fine without me, I bid them farewell and made my way along the short path from the stables to the castle.

I loved the castle even more in the dead of night when none but me lay awake, and I was free to roam its halls undisturbed or watched. The castle would never belong to me in the way it would someday belong to Alasdair, but in the moments when I moved through its corridors unaccompanied by watchful eyes, it felt like I was its mistress. My affection for its stone walls and elegant beauty knew no bounds.

I approached the door to my bedchamber with growing weariness as I considered just how shameful it would be to crawl into bed without changing out of my dress. As long as I woke early, none would be the wiser. It sounded delightful.

Opening the door and slipping inside, I walked through the room's darkness picturing my impending dreams as I crawled on top of my blankets still fully clothed.

A sudden rustling sound near the window caused my head to whip in its direction. The shadowy figure of a man stood not far from my bed.

With no hesitation, no worry over what practicing magic in front of another might do, I flicked my wrist and sent the candles scattered around my room blazing with light.

At once, the man was revealed.

"Rab?"

The young man glanced around the room with horror.

"'Tis true, then. Ye really are a witch."

He held the small chest which contained the jewels I wore only on the most special of occasions in his hands.

"And ye are a thief. If ye mean to imply that my crime is worse than yer own, ye will surely find that my father would disagree. Unless ye wish me to call for him, ye will place my

41

chest back where ye found it, and ye will sit on the ground at once."

Every last detail slipped into place inside my mind as a plan took form.

He was quiet, brave, and foolish. If Rab could so easily sneak into my room without anyone else in the castle seeing him, then surely he could do the same in my father's bedchamber.

He would either steal Grier's books for me, or my father would learn of his crime.

The choice was his.

Chapter 5

Three glorious weeks of learning passed in a blur of sleepless nights and hazy days.

As expected, Rab eagerly agreed to steal the books to avoid whatever punishment my father would have cast upon him. Within two days of finding Rab, jewel chest in hand, every last journal was hidden away in my room. I spent every night working my way through the dozens of journals. It would take time—years even—to perfect the various spells found within, but I was willing to spend the time to have such power at my disposal.

In order to avoid suspicion, I only dared open the books once in my bedchamber for the evening. I would stay up long into the night reading and practicing until my eyes would close of their own accord. I was exhausted, happy, and terrified. The missing books wouldn't go unnoticed forever, and I knew that after having seen the learning available to me within Grier's books, I would never be able to go back to a life without them.

On the day Alasdair returned from his mysterious journey, as we sat down for our first family dinner in months, the inevitable occurred.

"Mary." Father's voice was harsh as he motioned for her to stay in the room after seeing the banquet of food she'd prepared and set before us.

"Aye, sir? Is there anything else ye wish me to bring ye?"

He shook his head and continued.

"No, there is more here than we could eat in a fortnight. Once our meal is finished, I want ye to have every servant within and around the castle brought here to the dining hall. I've a matter I wish to discuss with all of ye."

Mary hid her concern well and nodded obligingly before turning to leave.

The moment we were alone, Alasdair spoke. He looked tired and troubled. I knew something more tugged at him than what Father had just said.

"Ye've never gathered everyone together before. What's happened?"

"We've a thief amongst the servants. A great many books have gone missing from my chamber. I intend to find who took them and why. I shall see them freed of their hands."

I swallowed and glanced down at my lap in a panic as I thought of Rab. Death would be preferable to the loss of one's hands among the poor. For without hands to work with, a slow and painful death of starvation was bound to follow.

"Books? What need would a servant have of books? Most of them canna read." Alasdair's voice was disbelieving. "'Tis possible they've been misplaced. When ye sent me to yer chamber before I left, I couldna find the letter ye sent me looking for. Ye keep yer chamber in a dreadful state."

Anger flashed in Father's eyes, and his fist rattled against the table.

"I dinna misplace two dozen books. O'course I doona believe the thief stole the books to read them. They are rare and valuable—one could sell them for a high price amongst those of particular interests."

I sat in rigid silence unsure of which action would make me look more guilty—saying nothing and pretending that I couldn't hear them, or speaking up and joining in.

I glanced up and caught Alasdair's eyes and knew. My silence had already piqued his own suspicion of my involvement in this. I couldn't allow it to raise my father's.

"Particular interests? What are the books about, Father?"

He didn't bother to look at me as he answered.

"'Tis none of yer concern. Ye would all do best to take account of yer belongings. I doona believe my books can be the only stolen items."

The meal dragged on at a torturously slow pace. I couldn't eat another bite. All I wanted was to escape to my room where I could try to come up with a way to prevent my accomplice from being revealed.

Finally, when everyone else's eating slowed, Alasdair came to my rescue.

"Morna, I brought ye back a gift from my journey. If ye are finished eating, come with me so I may get it for ye."

Alasdair paused and turned to address our father.

"I'll join ye here when ye address them if ye wish it. It willna take the two of us long."

Father nodded, and I was up and out of my seat before he could change his mind. I knew I needed Alasdair's help, but all I could think of was the weariness on his face. Something had happened while he was away—something terrible.

I didn't wait until we made it to my bedchamber, instead turning toward him the moment we were a safe distance from the dining hall.

"What is it? Are ye injured?"

"No, I'm fine. What I wish to speak to ye about can wait. What have ye done, Morna? I can tell by looking in yer eyes, ye know of what Da speaks."

Nearing my room, I reached for my brother's arm and pulled him inside.

"The books father spoke of—they are Grier's spells and journals."

Alasdair's face reddened and his jaw clenched.

"I will never understand his fear of magic. 'Tis a blessing, not a curse, and 'tis dishonorable for ye to deny who ye are. How did ye learn he had them?"

I told him everything—of Eoin's discovery, of my pact with Rab, of everything I'd learned in the past weeks and of how I would run away from here before ever going without such knowledge again. When I finished, Alasdair stood in thoughtful silence for a long moment. When he finally spoke, his resolve was firm.

"Go and tell Father that Mae has sent word asking for yer help. He willna like it, but he will allow it. Tell him ye will be gone three days and that Kip will escort ye to the village. Then, go to Kip and tell him everything. Have him prepare three horses and pack enough for a three-day journey. Elspeth willna be pleased that I'm leaving again, but I doona see another way. I'll see to everything else."

"We're leaving?"

"Aye. Rab's guilt must come to light. Without someone to blame, Father will make life for the servants unbearable. Doona worry, I'll not allow Father to harm him. One way or another, we will see him safely to another territory."

"I must get the books hidden away before we leave. What if Father looks for them?"

Ahead of me, Alasdair nodded and shooed me from the room.

"I know just the place. I'll take them there myself. Go. Hurry. We've not much time. This is just the beginning of troubles we must discuss this night."

Before I could ask what he meant, Alasdair pushed me out into the hall and closed the door in my face.

"We'll stop here."

With the sun just peaking over the horizon, Alasdair abruptly pulled his horse to a stop. Rab and I quickly did the same. We remained a good distance from the nearest territory, and I wouldn't feel safe until we saw Rab away and settled from Conall land for good.

Alasdair dismounted effortlessly then moved to pull Rab from atop his horse as if he were nothing more than a small child. Confused, I called after him as he led the man away.

"What are ye doing? We should keep going. We…" I was left straddling my horse, Cadha, near an opening in the trees, staring after Alasdair as he attempted to lead Rab away from me.

Gently nudging Cadha, I moved to block their path.

"What do ye mean to do with him?"

Alasdair rarely lost his patience with me but exhaustion made him irritable.

"Even a man as foolish as him wouldna dare to step back into Conall territory after this night. There is no need to see him all the way to the next territory. I need to rest. I havena slept in days, and there is still much on my mind. We will bid farewell to Rab here."

The fear in Rab's expression was evident. Alasdair was right. Rab would never again cross over into my father's territory.

Tightening his grip on Rab's arm, Alasdair leaned in close, his voice a growl as he spoke directly to the thief.

"Had I allowed my father to do as he wished, ye would have had no hope for a future. Doona steal from another. See this as a chance to live a better life. And hear this—if word of what ye know about my sister spreads throughout this land in any way, I shall kill ye with my own two hands."

Pledging to change his ways and keep my secret, Rab ran away the moment my brother released his grip.

"Ye've more of Father in ye than ye show. Ye frightened even me."

Pulling a blanket from the top of his horse, Alasdair spread it on the ground and moved to lay on it. I could see from the weariness of his steps, he would be asleep within moments.

"Good. I meant every word. There is nothing in this world I wouldna do to protect ye, lass."

While Alasdair slept, I led each of the three horses to the small stream just beyond the forest clearing. More accustomed—thanks to my nights reading Grier's books—to being up until dawn, I wasn't as sleepy as my brother. I was, however, stiff and sore from riding through the night. Walking over to Cadha, I opened my pack to search for my own blanket in the hopes that I might spread it on the ground and rest my body for a while. My blanket was nowhere to be found.

"Are ye hiding it from me, Cadha? Or did Rab manage to take off with it?" Cadha neighed, and I took a moment to stroke her before moving over to Alasdair's horse. In the haste with which we left the castle, I assumed some of my belongings had been placed on one of the other horses.

As I reached inside Alasdair's pack, a small piece of parchment fluttered to the ground. Bending to pick it up, I struggled to make sense of the nearly unreadable hand. Slowly, I pieced the words together as my hands shook.

I found the home of the lass ye seek. I regret to inform ye of her recent death. Her home was set aflame by the laird of Kentrich territory. He believed her to be a witch. She perished in the fire.

I could think of only one person Alasdair would have gone in search of who would be accused of witchcraft. Alasdair's troubled expression suddenly made sense.

He believed Grier was dead.

I knew without doubt that she was not.

Chapter 6

A lasdair slept until midday. While I napped briefly, I spent most of my time impatiently tending to the horses. I wouldn't wake my brother—not when it was so clear how desperately he needed the rest—but it took every bit of willpower I possessed to keep from doing so. There were so many things we needed to discuss.

When at last I heard him stir, I left the horses and carried the small piece of parchment over to his blanket and plopped down in front of him, waving it in his face.

"Is Grier the lass to which this man refers?"

Still not fully awake, Alasdair stretched his exceedingly long legs and slowly pulled himself up to a seated position. His light brown hair fell in a mess of lovely waves around his shoulders. It was no wonder the female servants of the castle doted on him. Their ridiculous behavior made me hope I would never meet a man that turned me into such a fool.

After a few blinks, Alasdair seemed to realize both what I'd said and what I held in my hand. Regret etched his face as he spoke.

"Where did ye get that? 'Tis not the way I wished ye to learn of her death, lass. I'm so verra sorry."

I wanted to be certain before I said what I intuitively knew. I repeated my question.

"So Grier is the woman mentioned in this letter, aye?"

His eyes downward, Alasdair nodded.

"Aye, lass."

Waving the parchment excitedly, I smiled and laid it down in front of him.

"Whoever wrote this is wrong. Grier is no more dead than ye or I."

Interest piqued, my brother's brows pinched together as he leaned forward and stared at me.

"How can ye possibly know that?"

I wasn't sure, but I knew with absolute certainty that I was right.

"I still feel her somehow. 'Tis as if our shared magic bonds us in a way I doona have the knowledge to understand. Grier is still alive."

Alasdair took in breath so quickly that his lungs made a painful noise at the sudden intrusion of cold hair. Relief seemed to roll off him as I looked on in wonder.

I assumed Alasdair's distress had come from his worry over how I would handle the news of Grier's death, but I could see as I watched him that I had missed something in my assumption.

"I dinna know ye cared for Grier so much."

A half-hearted, restrained smile crossed my brother's face as he leaned back on his arms and looked across at me.

"Grier was the first woman I ever loved."

Still not understanding, I dismissed him.

"Everyone was in love with Grier."

"No, lass. Ye doona understand. I wanted to marry her. I asked her more than once but she denied me every time, never giving me an explanation that made any sense. She held my heart in a way that only Elspeth has ever surpassed."

My mind reeled. While a kinder sister would have been more sympathetic toward her brother's heartfelt confession, I couldn't help but find it anything other than hysterically funny.

"Alasdair, I know why she wouldna marry ye."

His brows lifted again as he twisted his head in doubt.

"Do ye now? Please, do tell."

"Grier is at least four times yer age—older than our grandmother was."

I bent over and lost myself in a fit of hysterics as Alasdair's eyes all but bulged from their sockets.

"Trust me, lass. I know that canna be true. I saw more of Grier than I had right to at such a young age, and there was no part of her that was aged in any way."

I struggled to speak between bouts of laughter as I lifted from my doubled-over position to look at him.

"Aye, 'tis true. Her magic allows her to appear whatever age she pleases. She told me that I would someday be able to do the same. We doona age like the rest of ye."

I watched Alasdair's face carefully change from an expression of horror to amusement. Before long, he sat laughing even more loudly than I was.

"I hardly know what to say. While I canna rightly express how pleased I am to hear that she is alive, I doona believe I'll ever be able to think of her in the same way again."

With my own laughter finally subsiding, other obvious questions came to mind.

"Why were ye looking for her, Alasdair? We've barely spoken of her since she left."

Alasdair's face grew grim once more as he corrected me.

"She dinna leave, Morna. I doona believe she ever would have left if Father hadn't sent her away. I saw her face that day in the field. It broke something in her—not only her heart but nearly her soul—to leave us that day. Ye've need of her now. I thought it past time I saw her home."

Alasdair always believed he knew more about what I needed than I did. Most of the time, he was right. The same age difference lay between me and Alasdair, as did between Alasdair and our father—sixteen years. Oftentimes, it seemed that while Father was Alasdair's da, Alasdair served as mine.

"Why do I have more need of her now than ever? Has something happened to me that I canna see?"

Alasdair let out a frustrated growl as he stood and paced in front of me.

"I knew he wouldna do it. He told me he would tell ye, but he's said nothing of what he's done, has he?"

"Father? No, I spoke little to him while ye were away. 'Tis usually best for me to keep my distance."

"He's sent for suitors, Morna. He expects ye to be wed by year's end. While I've no objection to ye marrying if ye wish to, and blessings to Mother for what she made him promise before her death, I doona believe men of Father's choosing should be pushed on ye."

Alasdair continued to stomp around in the field before me, speaking so quickly I had no chance to interject on any point.

"Ye are different than other women, Morna. Ye are special. Father will choose fools. There is little I can do to stop him from forcing yer hand in the direction he wishes it to go. If I was laird, I would protect ye. Ye'd be free to practice yer magic as ye wish it, and if ye never wished to marry, ye would have a home in my castle.

"I sent men in search of Grier in the hopes that she could return, and I could hide her away so that she could teach ye. That way, when ye are married, ye would at least have the aid of yer magic to ensure that ye lived yer life as ye wished it."

I thought back to that last day with Grier as Alasdair spoke. Though I spent little time thinking of marriage, I seemed far less frightened of it for myself than those around me.

When Alasdair finally exhausted himself from talking, I spoke.

"Is marriage so terrible? That day in the field—the last day we saw her—Grier warned me of the same thing."

With a reddened face and trembling hands, Alasdair joined me on the ground. Anger didn't suit him. My brother was good through and through.

"With the right partner, marriage can be a joy, but Morna, ye've been more sheltered than ye know by the life we've lived. Oftentimes marriage is a prison where women are abused and used and treated like property. And this is true for the plainest of women. For a lass like ye, for one with yer powers, the wrong sort of man would take advantage of yer abilities. If ye doona know how to control them, ye will be powerless to protect yerself from it. I suspect Grier knew that firsthand. What did she tell ye that day? And what was the spell Father interrupted? I've always wondered, though I think some part of me was too afraid to ask. While I know the goodness of Grier's soul, I always sensed a hint of darkness in her, hidden just beneath the surface of her smile."

I knew just what my brother meant. Even though I'd adored her growing up, even though I'd graciously accepted any knowledge she was willing to bestow upon me, there was a complexity of soul about her that always made me more nervous than I was willing to admit. Something about her frightened me deeply.

"I can scarcely remember, though I believe 'twas a love spell."

Alasdair's voice was incredulous.

"A love spell? At twelve?"

"No. She dinna mean for it to take place then. She was worried about who Da would choose for me later, just as ye are. I doona know what she meant to do. I canna remember her words, only a verra vague image of a man. 'Tis evident though that Father's interruption kept it from working. I've never seen the man in real life, and it seems 'tis too late if Father is inviting men of his choosing to the castle as we speak."

Alasdair nodded.

"I expect the first suitor will be there when we return. Doona allow Father to push ye toward any man ye doona love. While I can do nothing to keep him from seeing ye married, he promised Mother long ago that the choice of whom ye marry would be yers. So wait until ye find a man worthy of holding yer heart—a man who will never misuse yer powers. Da may be many things, but he does keep his word."

I didn't wish to think or talk about suitors. I knew nothing of love. How would I know when a man was worthy of holding my heart? My sheltered life had left me ignorant of so many things. While my discernment for the attractions in others' hearts seemed engrained in my nature, I had no faith in my ability regarding my own love life. I had so much to learn.

"Alasdair, will ye continue looking for Grier now that ye know she is not dead? I would give anything to speak to her now—to have her help in learning from her journals."

My heart sank as he shook his head.

"I willna leave ye alone with Father once the suitors arrive. For now, ye must use the books and the books alone to learn."

"Where did ye put the books before we left?"

It surprised me that I'd not spent every waking moment worrying over them until now.

"I've a surprise for ye when we return. There's no more need for ye to spend yer nights toiling over Grier's spell books in yer bedchamber. I've readied a place—a safe place—where ye can learn as much as ye wish. I'll make certain that Father never learns of its existence."

I threw my arms around him in gratitude. I never wanted to live in a world without Alasdair.

If one of Father's suitors could love me half as much as he did, I would consider myself lucky.

Chapter 7

Note from M.C.:

There is real magic in this world and not only the sort of magic that I possess. There is a greater magic, one that works in and around all of us—connecting us in a way that we may never fully understand.

And the source of this magic—mysterious it may be—has a wondrous sense of humor. As I hugged my brother's neck silently wishing that there might be one other man who could love me as much as him, something inside me didn't believe it possible. My limited experience truly led me to believe that Alasdair was the only great man left. How foolish the naïve can be.

Never doubt the abundance that's out there for you. Our world is big, and great, and wonderful.

When I thought all that lay before me was a life of mediocrity with a man perhaps only slightly better than my father, magic was already at work, all the while laughing at my lack of faith.

While I squeezed my brother's neck, the man I wished for lay only a few dozen yards away. Which brings me to the first part of our story where my husband decided that my voice simply wasn't enough. I have to say...he was right.

I've learned so many things about him through this process. For so long, I believed he detested me. In truth, he was simply scared to death by how much he cared.

Fear makes such fools of us all.

Jerry

F our hundred and eighty-five days is a long time for a man to remain trapped in a time other than his own. If not for my unrelenting belief that there must be a purpose to the strange happening—a reason why I was meant to visit this time—I would have lost my mind long ago. It was my faith in some sort of divine plan that kept me from giving in to the despair I knew would come if I allowed myself to believe that I would never again see my friends, my family, or my home.

With every passing minute, I inched closer to despair.

My mouth was so dry from going over twenty-four hours without even a drop of water that even breathing hurt my parched throat. For three months, I'd survived rather easily as a vagabond. With more farming knowledge than most in these parts, I was always handy enough to find short-term work that would pay me enough to see me to the next village.

Now, only one day's ride from my destination, I lay stuck in a shallow stream with one arm trapped between rocks and my other arm dislocated so horrifically that I couldn't move it at all.

The pain was terrible, but it was my inability to move enough to get myself a drink of water that would kill me.

While I was nowhere near death yet, if the travelers up ahead were anything like the last to come across me, I would be soon.

They couldn't see me. While I could tell they were speaking, they were too far away for me to make out any of their conversation despite the loud volume of their dialogue with one another. I knew they wouldn't be able to hear my dry and quiet voice if I called for them. All I could do was sit, wait, and hope that one of them would venture in my direction soon.

For the longest time, everything fell silent. I worried that the strangers had gathered their belongings and left in the opposite direction. Eventually, hours later, they stirred and proceeded to talk and laugh together for another series of hours that left me reeling in frustration. Had I the ability to speak, I would've screamed obscenities at them for being so careless.

None of this was their fault, of course. I knew that. But thirst and fear makes all thought irrational. I needed help. I needed it badly. If they left here without seeing me, I would die.

I couldn't die. Not here. Not in this time. Not without knowing the reason for my sudden appearance in the seventeenth century exactly four hundred and eighty-five days ago.

Exhaustion hit me in waves as I lay propped up in my immobile position in the stream. With water lapping over both legs, I would sleep for short periods on and off throughout the day. At some point, I drifted. When I finally opened my eyes, the scene in front of me was finally different.

Rather than the same old stream, the most beautiful pair of green eyes I'd ever seen bore into my own. Her palms grasped either side of my face as she spoke in a whisper.

"I canna wait to hear how this happened to ye. Doona faint. My brother is about to move yer shoulder into place. I imagine 'twill hurt. 'Tis hanging in an ungodly position."

Before I could brace for it, an unspeakable pain rushed up and through my arm as consciousness slipped away from me once again.

I didn't care.

I was saved, and in more ways than I could have possibly known at the time.

Chapter 8

Jerry, the strange disheveled man riding between my brother and me, would be fine. Thankfully, color returned quickly to his dislocated arm. Although it would be tender for weeks, it would heal. The condition of his other arm was remarkable as well. Caught in a rock fall that sent him slipping into the middle of the stream, the rock that held his right arm hadn't crushed any part of him. It had fallen in precisely the perfect position so that his arm fit snugly between two rocks. If not for the width of his hand, he would've been able to pull his arm through and free himself.

He was of average height but looked small next to my brother. His dark hair was cropped shorter than that of most men. While the length of his beard made him look older, I suspected that he was at least five years younger than my brother. He was dirty, smelled awful, and was so weary he could scarcely hold himself upright on his horse.

"Where were ye headed, lad? Were ye traveling alone? Why doona ye have any belongings with ye?"

Alasdair asked each question in such rapid succession that Jerry had no opportunity to respond. Each time the man opened his mouth to answer, my brother would send another question his way.

"Alasdair, why doona we see him to Mae's inn, allow him to rest a while and then speak to him? He canna wish to speak of any of this just now. Look at him."

Glancing over at me for the first time since we began the ride back to Conall territory, the stranger gave me a thankful, shy smile before turning to speak to Alasdair.

"Aye, forgive me, but the lass is right. My arm aches and I'm weary. If ye will see me to somewhere that I may rest for the night, I will answer anything ye wish to ask me come morning. I've little in means, but I'll find some way to repay yer kindness."

Alasdair nodded and ashamedly looked down.

"There is nothing to repay. O'course ye doona wish to talk. Forgive my rudeness. Can ye reach inside the pack to yer left? I believe there's a strong ale within that will surely help with the pain. Every drop inside is yers."

My brows lifted as I leaned forward and looked over at my brother in surprise. Alasdair hated ale. I'd only seen him drink it in front of our father. Even then, he only did so to prevent Father's teasing.

Alasdair could see what I was thinking right away.

"'Tis not mine. Rab stowed it away."

Jerry started in on the ale as if it were his first drink of water after we freed him.

He would be sick with drink by the time we reached Conall territory.

Alasdair and I returned to Mae's inn before the sun rose the next day. Wayward travelers were common in Scotland. While this wasn't the first time someone in my family had offered help to one of them, Jerry piqued my interest more than most.

It wasn't just his short hair and the oddity of the predicament we'd found him in that intrigued me—there was a familiarity about his eyes that I couldn't quite place.

Even drunk, Jerry had remained kind and courteous to us both, and I suspected that it was this that made Alasdair as eager as me to check on him the next day. Accustomed to men growing boisterous and misbehaving after drinking, the man's ability to maintain his dignity impressed my brother greatly. I'd even heard him speak to Kip about hiring the man on as the new stable hand if he was in need of work.

When we arrived at the inn, Mae was already busy at work in the kitchen, though no guests were down from their rooms yet.

"Is he awake?"

She nodded and answered my brother in a whisper.

"Aye, I believe so. I heard movement from within his room before I came down."

Following my brother, I stood back and waited while Alasdair ensured that Jerry was indeed awake and decent. When we walked inside, he looked as if he'd been expecting us for some time.

Alasdair wasted no time before asking his first question.

"Before the friendship between ye and my family continues, I must make certain that ye are not a man of ill-gotten means. Are ye a thief? Are ye on the run from anyone?"

65

I knew Alasdair didn't believe this man was any sort of criminal, but his question didn't surprise me. Alasdair was fiercely protective of the land that would one day be his and the people who lived on it.

"No, I survive by honest work and honest work alone. I held work at Creedrich Castle for the last year as a messenger for the laird. While I know that the circumstances in which ye found me doona speak to my talents, I know Scotland's land as if it were all my own."

"Are ye on an errand for the laird now? Were ye meant to deliver a message when ye fell?"

Jerry's beard made it difficult to discern much emotion from his expression, but I thought anger flashed in his eyes.

"No. I no longer offer my services to the laird of Creedrich territory. The man killed the...my..."

He hesitated and Alasdair pressed him.

"Yer what, lad?"

"My wife."

For the first time since meeting Jerry, I suspected him of lying. The word didn't flow from his mouth naturally. Instead his gaze dropped to the floor, and the word *wife* seemed to trip out of his mouth as if it had been pushed outward. The words hadn't been easy for him to say.

"Yer wife? Why would the laird kill yer wife?"

Jerry hesitated then stood up from the edge of the bed where he'd been sitting.

"I am sorry. I appreciate yer kindness in seeing me here, but I'm afraid 'tis not ye that I need to tell my story to. I must speak to the laird's son, for he is the only one who may be able to help me. Do ye know how I might cross his path?"

Casting me a careful glance, Alasdair crossed his arms and joined me against the wall.

"The laird's son? Do ye know him?"

Jerry shook his head.

"No, though my...my wife," again he seemed to struggle with the words, "she knew him. I have reason to believe he tried to seek her out before her death. I mean to find out why."

Every hair on my body stood on end. He couldn't possibly mean Grier. Twisting to look at my brother, I watched as he tried to mask his thoughts. Alasdair was an open book—he looked as speechless as I felt. Silently asking Alasdair to stay back, I placed my hand on his arm and stepped away from the wall as I went to stand in front of Jerry. I wanted to look in his eyes as I asked him.

"The lass ye speak of—she is not yer wife, is she?"

He stared at me for a long, silent moment, and the same strange sense of déjà vu I'd felt while on horseback yesterday evening swept over me.

"Ye can tell me. If ye lied about it, I know there must be a reason."

While I meant for my words to put him at ease, I could see in the way that his gaze hardened, I'd only aroused his suspicion. Leaning back to increase the space between us, he didn't break eye contact as he answered me.

"Lass, if ye are of the opinion that I owe ye any explanation, ye are wrong. While I'm thankful for both of ye, this here is not what I owe ye. Name yer price in regard to the work I must do for ye. As soon as strength returns in my arms, I shall complete it and call the debt I owe ye paid. Now, I would appreciate it if ye would both leave me. I shall find a way to speak to the laird's son on my own."

Laughing, Alasdair stepped away from the wall. While Jerry's response only infuriated me, I could see by my brother's expression it only endeared the man to him even more. Alasdair would've behaved in exactly the same way had their roles been reversed. Jerry didn't know that he was standing in the same room with the very man he wished to find. He only knew that the two people who'd provided him aide were questioning him as if he were their prisoner.

"Lad, ye doona owe us anything. I believe I can help ye gain access to the man ye seek. I know the laird's son verra well. Ye said before that ye no longer offer yer services to the laird of the territory from which ye came. Are ye in need of work? Not debtors work, but work in which ye may earn yer keep to stay here?"

Jerry nodded. "Aye. Any work ye can offer me, I will happily take."

Alasdair smiled, and I could sense what he meant to do. It would please him to trick the man.

"I've no work for ye, but the castle's stable is looking for a new hand. I've business I must attend to with the laird himself this evening. I shall present ye to him. If he thinks ye suitable, perhaps he will allow ye to stay on. If ye work at the castle, ye are bound to cross paths with the laird's son. Ye can then reveal everything to him that ye doona wish to reveal to us."

Jerry smiled.

"Thank ye. Yer understanding and kindness means much."

Satisfied with himself, Alasdair moved to the door.

"Ye canna come to the castle looking like that, lad. Ye must see yerself cleaned and groomed if ye wish the laird to grant ye work."

With his left shoulder still bound to his chest and his right arm bruised, he would need help.

"I doona think he can. Will it really matter?"

With a horrified expression that I knew full well was pretend, Alasdair twisted in the doorway and looked back at me.

"Aye, it matters. I willna bring any man before the laird and present him as my guest looking as he does now. What would the laird think of me?"

Shaking my head to shame him, I neared my brother and whispered, "What do ye expect him to do?"

Dismissively, Alasdair shrugged as we walked into the hallway.

"Mae can help him."

Mae constantly had more to handle than any person should ever have to. I wouldn't allow Alasdair to place one more burden on her shoulders.

"No. Say nothing to Mae. I'll see him shaved and readied for this charade of yers. Ye should be ashamed of yerself, Alasdair."

Alasdair laughed.

"Ye can tell him if ye like. Doona take long with him. Father will wish to see ye when ye return to the castle. He believes that ye've been here helping Mae, and ye know he will tell ye that he doesna care for it."

I had no wish to spend more time with the man than necessary. I wanted to return to the castle so I could see the surprise Alasdair mentioned the day before.

"Aye, I know. Go on. I'll follow ye shortly."

A few moments later, I returned to Jerry's room with a blade and bowl of water in hand. He eyed me skeptically.

"I've no desire to rid myself of my facial hair."

"Are ye in need of work? If so, I doona believe ye have a choice."

Pointing to a wooden seat in the room's corner, I waited for him to sit. He held out a hand to stop me as I approached.

"Wait. If ye mean to put a blade to my throat, I must at least know yer name first."

Setting the water bowl down on the table next to him, I reached forward to comb through the hair with my fingers. It was wiry and filthy. I couldn't wait to see what he looked like without it.

"I canna believe it dinna occur to ye to ask our names before now. 'Tis yer own fault my brother has fooled ye so. My name is Morna Conall, and the man who just offered to present ye to the laird is my brother, Alasdair—the laird's son."

Enjoying the look of embarrassed horror in his eyes, I set about my work.

Chapter 9

"Now that ye know who I am, ye might as well tell me the truth. The lass ye spoke of before...her name was Grier, aye?"

For the first part of his grooming—while I messily sawed away at the length of hair extending from his face—Jerry said nothing to me. Eventually, I couldn't stand it. I wanted to know everything. How did he know Grier, and why was he still under the impression that she was dead?

Surprised, he glanced up at me, and I had to look away. The more I looked at his eyes, the more familiar they felt to me, and I found it difficult to maintain eye contact with him.

"Did ye know her?"

Tossing a length of hair onto the floor, I nodded. I knew I needed to be careful about what I revealed to him. While he gave the impression that he and Grier were quite close, I knew it wasn't safe to assume that he knew about her magic.

"Aye. She was one of my grandmother's dearest friends. I spent much time with Grier when I was younger."

This seemed to surprise him, and I knew that I'd been wise to say nothing of her magic.

"Friends with yer grandmother? She canna be that much older than ye are."

Twisting to clean the blade to ready it for application to his face, I smirked to myself. Grier never told men the truth about her age. If she did, she'd have a much harder time seeing them to her bed.

A flash of this man entangled with Grier flew unbidden into my mind. While I had no reason to have any feelings about such an image, I found it immensely displeasing.

Ignoring his statement about her age, I asked the same question I'd asked him earlier.

"Were ye truly married to her?"

Confirming my suspicions, he shook his head just one half motion to the right as I reached to steady his chin to clean away the first full strip of hair.

"Why did ye tell us that ye were?"

With one run of the blade completed, he seemed convinced that I didn't intend to slit his throat. He visibly relaxed.

"In truth, I canna believe yer brother left ye alone to tend to me. Had I known him to be so openminded, I might have told ye the truth. Grier and I were never married, though I lived with her for the past year."

Intrigued and far less offended than pretty much any other person in Scotland would be, I pressed further.

"My father would never stand for it, but Alasdair allows me my freedom. He believes I have a mind of my own."

Jerry surprised me by letting out a soft sigh. Under his breath, he whispered, "Aye, I doona doubt it."

"Ye dinna marry Grier, but ye loved her, aye?"

I would tell him that she lived soon enough. First, I wanted to hear his story to learn if there was a reason for Grier to purposefully make him believe she was dead.

"As a sister, aye. Grier and I were not together. Before she died, she was helping me find my way home."

The man was full of contradictions. First Grier was his wife. Now, he cared for her as a sister. First he said he knew Scotland as if all its land belonged to him. Now he said that he needed help finding his way home.

He was a mystery—one I was intent upon solving.

Pulling my blade back across his cheek to rid it of stubble, I questioned him.

"Yer way home? I thought ye knew Scotland's lands well."

He sighed deeply and reached to grab my arm. Gently pulling it away from his face, he continued to direct the blade back to the table.

"Wait a moment. I doona wish to tell ye while ye hold the blade. 'Tis probable ye will believe me mad, and I doona wish ye to open one of my veins in fear."

Unsettled by the touch of his hand, I pulled away and set the grooming instruments down. Moving to lean against the bed, I nodded in agreement and waited for him to begin. He looked ridiculous with the length of his beard jaggedly chopped and one clean strip of face showing across his right cheek. He didn't seem to notice or care.

"I risk much by telling ye, but I know that I must. If ye knew Grier, I have to hope that ye knew of her secret. If ye did, ye might know of a way to help me. Do ye know Grier's secret?"

So he did know of her magic, and he had need of it.

"Do ye mean to ask me if I knew Grier was a witch? Aye."

73

Relief flooded Jerry's face as a rush of anxiety-laced air left his lungs.

"Ach, thank God for it. If yer family truly doesna share the same fear as so many in the Highlands, perhaps yer father and brother can help me as I've hoped."

Nothing he could've said would have annoyed me more. Why did he assume that they would be the ones that could help him? Did he believe all I was capable of was shaving his mangy beard? Father would be enraged if he ever learned this man had even heard Grier's name. While I knew Alasdair would be sympathetic, he would be useless. Jerry sat in the room with the only person who could possibly help him, and he dismissed me because of my age and gender.

Perhaps, he'd been right to ask me to set the blade down.

"Ye'd be wise to never mention a word of this to my father. He's gone to great lengths to ensure that no memory of Grier remains in Conall territory. If ye show him that ye were acquainted with her, the kindest ye can hope for from him is banishment."

"But I thought ye said yer family knew she was a witch? Why would yer brother send for her if yer father disapproved of it?"

"Just as I have a mind separate from that of the men in my life, so does Alasdair have a mind separate from our father's. 'Twould be foolish of ye to believe that any of my father's beliefs align with my own."

I paused, the words I so desperately wanted to say stopping at the edge of my tongue.

I could almost hear Alasdair's protective voice boom in the outer regions of my mind urging caution. There was no reason for me to trust him, no reason for me to reveal to him that I too, had magic, but as I looked across at him, no part of me worried that I would be putting myself at risk. I wanted to tell him if only to make him feel badly for dismissing my ability to help him.

"Alasdair sent for Grier because he believed I needed her help. I'm a witch, too."

Jerry's reaction was not what I expected.

Smiling so that every one of his teeth showed, Jerry doubled over and laughed.

Chapter 10

Jerry

I laughed at the coincidence, not because I disbelieved her. After tumbling backwards through time and living with a witch for over a year, nothing should have surprised me.

I realized too late that my reaction angered Morna. With one quick flick of her wrist, the bonny lass extinguished the candles around the room, though it did little to darken the space around us. The sun was now up and shining through the small window behind her.

"Lass." I stood and reached for her, grabbing both hands. I lowered my head so she would look into my eyes. "I believe ye. I dinna laugh because I thought ye were lying. I laughed because sometimes I canna believe the oddity of my life. Now, please, finish what ye started here on my face. I must look a frightful mess."

She watched me carefully and eventually pulled away to move to the washbowl and blade. I resumed my seated position and awaited her touch. Her hands were gentle across my skin, and it took everything in me not to tremble at the light touch of her fingers.

"I canna see how ye thought it funny."

I waited until she finished one long stroke down my cheek, then spoke.

"Aye, well, if ye'd lived the past year of my life, perhaps ye would see the humor in it—dark though it may be. Can ye do more with yer magic than extinguish fire? I'm in need of great help."

I meant the question as a joke. If Grier had mentored her, the lass surely had great power, but as I watched her teeth clench, I fell silent.

"I…sometimes I can sense things that others cannot."

Astonishment in my voice, I twisted to look up at her as I spoke. "Is that all? Surely, it canna be."

Her next pull of the blade across my skin held more pressure than those before it. I could feel her anger in the way she held my chin.

"Did ye not hear me tell ye that my father sent Grier away from here? He doesna approve of magic. I've had no training in the use of my powers since I was twelve."

Shaking my head as she cleaned the blade, I reached to feel the bare half of my face. I'd not shaved since before my tumble through time.

"I doona think I care for yer father. He's allowed ye to become entirely useless."

The blade dropped against the table with a loud clank before I realized the stupidity of my words. They were thoughtless and selfish and below me. No matter how desperate I was to return home, it was unforgiveable for me to behave as if anyone owed me help.

I turned toward Morna slowly, expecting to see tears fill her eyes, or at the very least for her to rear back in shock. Instead, I watched as a brief flicker of pain crossed over her eyes—pain she quickly masked with the expertise of someone well practiced at being on the receiving end of an insult. It made me dislike her father even more. My hateful words weren't the first time this lass had been made to feel useless. I couldn't remember ever feeling so despicable.

Recovering quickly, she picked up the blade. While her voice was softer, she kept it steady.

"Aye, I know. Turn yer chair around so I may reach the other side of yer face."

Unsure how to apologize without making matters worse, I silently stood and did as she asked. We remained silent for what seemed like ages as she worked on my face. Finally, as she pulled the blade across one last time, I spoke.

"I doona think ye are useless, Morna. I'm just a frustrated fool who has been away from home for far too long. I verra much wish for us to be friends. Forgive me."

She stood behind me and said nothing as she reached around to brush the last bits of hair from my face.

The smile back in her voice, she patted my shoulders as she urged me to stand.

"There is nothing to forgive. Every word ye said was true. Now stand and introduce yerself to me. Ye no longer resemble the man I met yesterday."

Brushing hair from my kilt, I stood and faced her. Her mouth fell open, and she paled.

"Do I look that bad, lass?"

While I knew I must look different, her response seemed strange. More than shock appeared in her expression. She looked deeply shaken.

Afraid she might fall, I reached forward and grabbed her hands to steady her. She pulled away immediately and backed to the other side of the room.

"Why is it that ye are always reaching for my hands? Ye are more familiar with yer touch than ye have a right to be."

Smiling inwardly at her blush, my pulse quickened. She didn't mind my touch, and the realization bothered her. While the lass was still very much a stranger, the complexity of her character intrigued me.

She carried herself with the maturity of women twice her age, yet sometimes she would do or say something that revealed how young she truly was.

"I'm sorry if I've offended ye, lass. 'Tis only that ye look quite troubled."

She pointed to the seat behind me. Understanding her silent command, I turned the chair around once again and sat. The moment I was seated, she spoke.

"I need ye to tell me everything about yer relationship with Grier. Why was she helping ye? How did ye meet her? Alasdair canna help ye with this. Useless as I am, I am yer only hope."

Her reminder of my thoughtlessness pained me, but I knew it best to say nothing else of it and answer the questions she'd asked of me. While the possibility of her being able to see me home seemed small, I knew it was the only option I now had.

"Ye may verra well not believe my story, but I beg ye to listen silently until the end."

Agreeing with one small nod of her head, I continued.

"Lass, I canna explain what happened to me. I've yet to find anyone that can, but there is truth in every word I'm about to tell ye. I was not born in this century, not even in the next. My life, my friends, my family—they all lay in the twentieth century, some three hundred years in the future."

Pausing, I searched Morna's eyes but found her gaze unreadable. I continued.

"On the eve of my twenty-eighth birthday, I went to sleep inside my old farm house, content in knowing that come morning, I would have another long day of work ahead of me. I woke in the middle of the woods, far from my home, and entirely out of my time.

"I wandered for days until I reached a village outside of Creedrich Castle. It was only then that I truly began to realize the oddity of my circumstance. I believed I'd gone mad. No modern means of transportation lined the streets. No buildings resembled the town I knew from back home. I hid silently amongst the people for the better part of a week, eating scraps where I could find them, listening in on every conversation I could. Eventually, when I came to terms with the only reality I could imagine, I made a plan to ensure my survival.

"Even out of my own time, I knew that I could navigate Scotland. So I went to the laird to offer my services as a messenger. I hoped that by traveling I could find someone who could help me home. I dinna have to look far. 'Twas at the castle, I met Grier."

For the first time since beginning my long tale, Morna spoke. "Did Grier work for the laird?"

I shook my head.

"No. The laird of Creedrich Castle, like yer father, fears magic. His wife doesna share his fear. Grier would often provide healing remedies to the lady of the castle in secret. The night I went to offer my services to the laird, Grier was sneaking away from the lady's bedchamber.

"I said nothing to her that night and was hired on as a messenger like I hoped. 'Twas only after working at the castle for some weeks that I began to hear rumors of Grier's work within the castle. Eventually, I thought it worth the risk to seek her out and tell her my story. She believed me immediately and offered to help me return home.

"In short time, Grier and I secretly moved in together as 'twas easier for us to work on possible spells and read through old spell books together. Grier worked night and day trying to find a way to send me home, but in the year I was with her, we found nothing."

"Where were ye when Grier died?"

Memory of that terrible night still caused the breath to tighten in my chest. I couldn't bear to think of my friend dying in such a horrible way, and the guilt I felt for not being there weighed on me every single day.

"I was away delivering messages for the laird. I know little of what happened. Only that I returned to find our home destroyed. When I made my way to the village, I was told that the laird found out about his wife's friendship with Grier and attempted to banish her for witchcraft. When she refused to leave, he set our home aflame. Rather than abandon her home, she allowed herself to burn inside."

It was this that made my grief easier to bear. While I missed her, I couldn't bring myself to forgive her for leaving me. Her pride sentenced me to a life out of time.

"I'm sorry."

Morna's small voice pulled me from my thoughts.

"Aye. 'Twas the darkest night of my life. In my rage, I left Creedrich territory and traveled aimlessly for months seeking work and keeping an open ear for another with magic who might help me. A fortnight ago, I crossed paths with yer brother's messenger. When I learned he sought Grier, I knew I needed to come to Conall territory. I hoped that if ye all knew Grier, ye might know of a way to help me. It seems I was right. Will ye help me, Morna?"

Slowly, Morna walked across the room, never glancing in my direction as she spoke.

"I must think, Jerry. I'll see ye this evening."

Without another word, the only other person I'd ever told my tale to walked away. Her quick retreat was enough proof of her disbelief.

She thought me mad.

Dinner with her father was now more important than ever. I needed Morna's help even if it took me years to convince her that my story was true. Work at the castle would keep me close to her.

I would stop at nothing to win the trust of Morna's bastardly father.

Chapter 11

Morna

I made the walk back to the castle in half the time it normally took. I was still shaking by the time I entered through the castle's main doors. While shaving the second half of Jerry's face, he was turned away from me. The moment he stood and faced me, I knew why I found his eyes so familiar. Every memory of my last day with Grier returned at once.

Jerry was the man in the mirror—the man Grier intended to find for me.

My emotions swung wildly from disbelief to fear to anger. Due to Father's interruption that day, I assumed her spell hadn't worked. Did Jerry's sudden presence in my life mean it had? Could his story of being born in another time possibly be true?

There were stories in Scotland—legends of people taken by fairies, only to be returned to a time very different from that which they left—but this was different. Could witches manipulate time, as well?

So much of Jerry's story made little sense. If he was indeed the man Grier intended to bring me, why did she allow him to live with her for a year after she found him? And if he truly did fall through time, it was Grier who caused him to do so. Why then, had she pretended to not know how to send him home? Furthermore, why had she led him to believe she was dead? Did she know that she could no longer pretend to be ignorant of the aid he so desperately needed and worried of his reaction once he found out she'd been lying to him?

No, that couldn't be it—Grier feared no one.

The questions in my mind only seemed to build on themselves. In my distracted state, I didn't hear my father's voice until he called to me a second time.

"Morna, dinna ye hear me? Come here, lass."

His voice caused any thought of Grier or Jerry to vanish. Any interaction with my father required my focused attention. I could never allow myself to fall behind in conversation with him. Whenever I did, it ended with me being pushed into something I didn't want.

Smiling as sweetly as I could manage, I apologized and made my way over to him.

"I'm sorry. The past days at the inn have tired me. If ye'll excuse me, I'd like to rest before dinner. Thank ye for allowing me to offer Mae aid."

My efforts to dismiss my father rarely worked, but it never stopped me from trying. I turned away as he called me back to him.

"Ye may rest shortly. What I have to tell ye willna take long."

Father's tone made me nervous—there was more patience in his voice than usual—a sure sign that he was after something. Moving to sit in the chair opposite him by the fire, I feigned concern. If Alasdair's warning the day before was correct, I already suspected what our impending conversation was about.

"What is it? Has something happened?"

"No, I've good news. 'Tis time for ye to choose a husband."

I chose my next words carefully. If I wanted him to keep the promise he'd made my mother, I couldn't anger him with my response.

"'Tis time for me to choose? Surely, ye would be better suited to choose whom I should marry?"

The words tasted like bile on my tongue.

As I knew he would, Father said nothing of his promise. Instead, he wished to make me believe allowing me a choice in my future was a show of his generosity towards me.

"Ye are to make yer own choice, though I shall invite suitors of my choice here. The first suitor is already here as my guest. He shall join us at dinner. If after meeting this man and spending time with him, ye canna see yerself wed to him, we will send for another."

He paused, and I could see by the way he looked away from me and into the fire that he wasn't finished.

"Morna, I trust ye know that what I am allowing ye is unusual. Most men wouldna allow it."

He wanted me to thank him. Doing so would cost me nothing. I could thank him and then send each and every suitor away. Eventually, perhaps he would grow tired and relinquish his quest to see me married.

It wasn't that I never wanted to marry, but like Alasdair, I wanted to understand the power within me before I relinquished my freedom to another.

Putting on the mask I always wore in front of my father, I stood, smiled, and moved to kiss his cheek.

"Thank ye, Father. Yer kindness means more to me than ye can possibly know."

Wiping my lips with the back of my hand, I went in search of the one person I knew could help me sort through all that Jerry had told me—Alasdair.

"**M**ary, just give me one wee taste. What harm will it do? I willna tell a soul ye allowed me to taste it early."

I could hear Alasdair the moment I reached the first step leading down to the castle's kitchen. Mary's banter with everyone was entertaining, but she and Alasdair shared a special bond of friendship that made it even more so.

"Alasdair, if ye doona believe I shall stick ye with this poker if ye doona step away from the fire, I shall be happy to prove ye wrong. Elspeth willna be pleased if ye wind up with an arse that's so sore ye canna walk for days."

"Mary!"

I stepped into the room, but neither of them seemed to notice me.

"Doona 'Mary' me. Yer own mouth is far more foul than my own. Ye think that ladies doona think the same foul words that ye men say every damned day. Well, we do. 'Tis only that I know ye too well to worry over what I say in front of ye."

"I know ye well, and I've never known ye to speak in such a way. Something is bothering ye."

I knew exactly what bothered her, but I said nothing as I waved when Alasdair glanced my way.

Following Alasdair's gaze, Mary ran over to hug me the moment she saw me.

"Morna, I feel I havena seen ye in years. Where were ye? I know ye were not with Mae as yer father believes."

"I'll tell ye later. Will ye allow me to speak with Alasdair alone for a moment?"

Pulling away, she crossed her arms and glared at me.

"Ye canna mean to send me from my own kitchen?"

Apologetically, I reached forward to squeeze her arm.

"Aye, I am. I'll make it up to ye. 'Twill only take a few moments."

Something about my tone must have expressed my urgency, as she left the kitchen without another word.

When we could no longer hear footsteps, Alasdair spoke.

"I came here to wait for ye. I knew ye would come to the kitchen after returning from the inn. I'm afraid I have terrible news."

"Aye, I know. I've already spoken to Father. He told me the first suitor is already here. Who is he?"

Alasdair's nose crinkled upward in disgust, which only affirmed what I already suspected. My father's opinion of me was so low he'd invited trolls into our home to woo me.

"His name is Fulton Fyfe. His father is laird of a small territory. I believe Father only summoned him here because he wishes to control that territory once Fulton's father passes. The man is weak. He would happily allow Father to run his territory. Ye willna care for him, but news of the suitor is not the terrible news I have for ye."

My already knotted stomach tightened further.

"What is?"

"I no longer have a place where ye can practice yer spells. The room I planned for ye is where Father placed the suitor. I hid the books in my own chambers until I think of another way."

Even unintentionally Father could destroy my hope. I had no time to worry over it now.

"Alasdair, I must tell ye what I learned from Jerry."

Repeating every detail of my conversation, I told my brother everything. By the time I finished, Alasdair was pacing the room while rubbing his forehead.

"By all the saints, Morna, what are we to make of it?"

"I doona know. Why would Grier pretend that she couldna send him back? Why has she allowed him to believe her dead for so long?"

Ignoring my questions, he asked one of his own.

"Did ye tell him she's not dead?"

"Mayhap I should have, but I feared 'twould hurt him. He's been through so much already."

Alasdair stopped his pacing. His voice was low and quiet when he spoke.

"I told ye of the darkness I always sensed in Grier. I worry that the lass we knew is no longer the lass she is. There is a game in this that I canna understand. Whether it be loneliness or revenge, there is a design to all of it, and Grier is its creator. Ye must tell Jerry she lives. Yer memory is proof that he is at the center of all of it. He canna remain ignorant of what ye know."

"So, ye believe I must try to help him?"

Nodding, Alasdair leaned close as if he were worried Grier was listening to us even now. Part of me wondered if she was.

"Aye, ye must. I will find another place for ye to study and learn. If Grier lives, we will see her again. I will find her and see her home. We must learn the truth."

Shivering and exhausted, I readily accepted my brother's open arms.

"Only days ago, I feared I would go mad from boredom. Now, I fear there is too much chaos. Change is coming for me, and I doona know if I'm ready."

Holding me tight, Alasdair kissed the top of my head.

"Lass, ye are ready. Ye always have been. Ye are far more ready than I. I feel that yer life—the life ye were meant to live—is just beginning. I will miss ye terribly when ye leave here."

Teasing him, I pulled away and jerked my head toward the stairs.

"'Tis time for me to begin my life with Fulton, ye mean?"

Shivering, my brother took my arm as we left the kitchen together.

"Lass, if ye marry that fool, I shall never speak to ye again."

Laughing, we walked up the stairs, right into the path of my first suitor.

Chapter 12

Alasdair included nothing of Fulton's appearance in his description. In my mind, I imagined that I would arrive at dinner to find a horrendously unattractive man twice my age. To my surprise, when I found my feet after running right into him, I looked up into the eyes of one of the most handsome men I'd ever seen in my life.

As tall as my brother, Fulton Fyfe had dark eyes, thick lashes and brows, and a full head of dark hair that made me want to reach up and run my fingers through it.

He looked as if he could command any room, but when he opened his mouth to speak, no words formed. He opened and closed his mouth three times before finally deciding to say nothing. Without a word, he turned and walked away.

"I told ye. Strangest man I've ever seen. I doona believe he's said more than five words since he arrived."

Upon sitting down to dinner, Alasdair and I were determined in our resolve to make certain that Father took to Jerry well enough to give him work in Kip's stables. I knew it would be difficult. By introducing Jerry to Father as if he were Alasdair's friend, Father would assume that Jerry was already an equal in class. To then ask Father for work would only arouse suspicion. I hoped Alasdair had something planned.

With Father at the table's end, and Alasdair, Elspeth, and Eoin lining one side, I sat awkwardly between Jerry and Fulton.

Mary prepared a banquet of food, and I found myself eating more than my stomach could possibly hold just to keep my hands and mouth busy throughout the awkwardness of our meal together. Elspeth busied herself with Eoin, Fulton said absolutely nothing, and Alasdair and I watched on with wide eyes as Jerry charmed our father as if he'd known him his entire life.

It had been months, possibly even years, since I'd seen my father get on with someone so well. It unsettled me. My father usually liked despicable people. Did the fact that Jerry got along with him so splendidly signal something about Jerry's character that I'd not seen during my limited interaction with him?

Most people, even those with strong personalities, would shrink a few inches in my father's presence. They would choose their words with care and never dared say anything that might upset him. Jerry didn't seem concerned with this at all. If anything, he sat up taller than he had at any other time I'd seen him. Not only did he say whatever came to his mind, he even dared to disagree with my father twice before the main course.

The more disagreeable and opinionated Jerry was, the more my father enjoyed him.

"Alasdair, why have ye never brought Jerry here before? I've never known ye to have such intelligent friends."

Quicker than I would've been had I been the one asked, Alasdair took the opportunity to guide the conversation toward our desired outcome.

"He stays verra busy, Father. Until recently, he served as Laird Creedrich's most trusted messenger. He has only lived in this region for a fortnight."

Returning his attention to Jerry, Father looked surprised.

"Why did ye leave?"

As if they'd coordinated everything beforehand, Jerry picked up right where Alasdair left off.

"I much prefer the landscape here. There are too many peat bogs near Creedrich's land. I've a taste for the beautiful, and Conall territory is the loveliest in Scotland."

Picking the most beautiful area in Scotland was a lot like deciding which finger you'd like to lose—impossible. But the obvious stroke of his ego allowed Father to overlook the absurdity of Jerry's explanation.

"O'course ye do. Ye are a man of fine taste. How do ye mean to live?"

"'Tis part of the reason I invited him here tonight, Father. As ye know, Kip is now in need of a new stable hand. I thought mayhap Jerry would be a fine choice."

"A stable hand? Jerry would go to waste with such work. If he was a trusted messenger to Creedrich, he can be a trusted messenger to me. He can stay in the castle's cottage."

Choking on my food in surprise, I coughed as Jerry slyly reached to pat me on the back. He couldn't have seemed any less shocked by my father's offer. Perhaps Jerry possessed magic, as well. Father's actions were so unusual that I was beginning to wonder if he were spelled. To suggest that a man he barely knew take on such a trusted position was strange enough. To then offer the same stranger lodging on castle grounds was unheard of. With the exception of those who worked directly in the castle, such as Mary, Father never concerned himself with where his workers made their home.

Jerry continued to beat at my back while he spoke.

"Ye are too generous. A stable job will suit me just fine. I'm sure ye already have a messenger."

"Aye, but he's rubbish. I insist. I'll not take no for an answer."

Quickly adjusting his tone to one of admonishment, Father addressed me just as Jerry ceased the inappropriate thumping on my back. "Morna, compose yerself. Have ye no manners?"

As Mary brought in the last course, Father pounded one fist on the table in excitement.

"Mary, ye've outdone yerself, lass. I hope ye've saved some of everything for yerself to enjoy later."

Fulton jumped at the noise, bumping the table so that his cup of ale sloshed out on the table. The expression on my father's face made it clear that he'd forgotten Fulton was even there.

"How can a man so tall disappear so completely? Why doona ye speak, man? Have ye said two words to my daughter all evening?"

Suddenly feeling rather sorry for him, I tried to dismiss it.

"'Tis fine, Father. Yer conversation with Jerry had us all captivated."

Waving a hand to silence me, Father raised his voice in anger.

"I dinna ask ye. Speak and answer me. Have ye said a word since she sat down next to ye?"

While Father couldn't see it from so far away, I could see Fulton's hands shake as he struggled to speak. His face was so red I thought I might cry for him.

"I...I...no."

"After dinner, gather yer things and tell yer men that ye will return home come morning. There is no sense in ye being here if ye canna even speak to the lass ye wish to wed. Morna is not a quiet woman, she canna wed a mute."

Never in my life had two such completely conflicting emotions in regard to my father filled me at once. I was mortified that he didn't seem to mind the pain his words caused Fulton, but I was also pleased to see that at least some part of my father did care about my future happiness.

Unable to say a word, Fulton nodded and looked down at the table in total humiliation. Satisfied, Father resumed his conversation with Jerry.

As all attention diverted away from the devastated man next to me, I whispered an apology. Every word was forward and inappropriate, but if they helped to ease Fulton's pain, I didn't care. Only half of what I told him was a lie.

"Fulton, I think ye one of the most handsome men I've ever seen. I believe my father is wrong—I'm sure I could be verra content with ye if we were married, but ye surely doona wish to have my father ordering ye around until he dies. Be glad that he's sent ye away. Know that ye always have at least one friend here at Conall Castle."

For the first time, he smiled, and his hands stopped shaking.

"Thank ye, lass."

Quickly reaching out to squeeze his hand, I smiled then turned my attention back to the rest of the table. I could only hope getting rid of future suitors would be just as easy.

Chapter 13

B y the time dinner ended, I was no longer sure I wanted to help Jerry. It turned my stomach to see my father so jubilant. Father was so eager to see Jerry settled that he and Alasdair left immediately after eating to see the cottage readied for Jerry's immediate use.

Despite my misgivings, I knew that Alasdair was right. We had to help him and he had to know that Grier was alive.

With Fulton away to pack up his belongings, only Jerry, Elspeth, Eoin, and myself gathered in the sitting room by the fire. With Eoin asleep in Elspeth's arms, her own eyes were slowly closing in sleep. Knowing that the time had come to tell him, I kissed my sweet nephew's forehead and moved to stand next to Jerry.

"I thought ye dinna care for my father."

One corner of his mouth pulled up into a smile, and my heart began to race. I didn't enjoy looking at him without his beard. Every time I did, my body reacted in strange, unfamiliar ways.

"I said I dinna care for him before I met him. Now that I've met him, I like him even less." He paused and leaned in close as he took a quick glance in Elspeth's direction. "But Morna, I need

99

yer help. Ye may not believe me now, but with time, I'll convince ye. I need to be close with yer father to get close to ye."

Leaning back to distance myself from him, I nodded.

"But, I do believe ye. 'Twas only that there was much to take in before. I'll help ye, but I dinna lie to ye before. I know little of magic. It could take me years to learn what I need to help ye."

He shrugged as if he'd expected twice that length of time.

"It could take me years to find another witch. I've faith ye will learn quickly. Though I must ask ye, how will ye learn now if ye were unable to learn before?"

It was a reasonable question, one which I myself worried over. It was precisely why I needed to tell him about Grier. Once he knew she lived, he might wish to leave here and go in search of her.

"I recently found all of Grier's old spell books and journals. Once Alasdair finds a place where I can read and work without fear of Father discovering it, I will devote everything to learning. It has been my only wish for years now. Jerry, before ye decide to stay here, I must tell ye something."

"I doona believe I have any choice in staying here anymore. I'm not certain yer father would permit it."

He said the words jokingly, but I wasn't altogether certain he was wrong.

"If ye decide to leave after I tell ye, Alasdair and I will see to it that ye are able."

"I can see no other place where I would have a greater chance of finding someone to help me. Tell me what ye must. It willna change my mind."

He needed to know, but I didn't want to tell him. Knowing would hurt him. Even as nervous as he made me, the last thing I wanted was to cause him pain.

"Grier is alive."

Jerry's teasing smile vanished, and he watched me carefully as if gauging my sincerity.

I remained expressionless as I waited for him to respond.

When he finally did, his tone was strained.

"Part of me has wondered. I never thought Grier the kind of person who would easily accept death. I canna understand it though. I...I thought her my friend. Why would she allow me to believe her dead?"

I shook my head. "I doona know. Will ye look for her?"

His voice didn't waver. "No. I will help yer brother find a place for ye to work, and together we will find a way to get me home. Thank ye for telling me."

"Alasdair believes we will see her again."

Father entered the room, and Jerry turned to walk away from me, speaking quietly over his shoulder as he went.

"I've no doubt of it, lass. Morna, do ye truly believe it a coincidence ye found her books only just before I arrived here? If ye thought Grier powerful when ye knew her, ye have no idea what she's capable of now."

I stared after him as he left, astonished that it hadn't crossed my mind before now.

Had Eoin really stumbled across the books all on his own?

Chapter 14

Two Months Later

With both Jerry and Alasdair eager to find a place for me to learn and work, it didn't take long for them to figure out a solution. It was much more perfect than I could've dreamed.

On the back side of the castle, hidden by years of foliage and dirt, was a door to a separate basement room in the castle. Empty for years, it was dirty and dark, but I couldn't have minded less. For despite the frigid air and damp walls, there was no reason for any of us to suspect that Father would have reason to enter it. It was private, and it was mine.

In order to allow me even more time to read through Grier's countless books, Alasdair hired a nurse for Eoin. While I missed my days spent in the child's company, I couldn't bring myself to feel guilty over being away from him. My enthusiasm allowed me to learn quickly. Within the month, I mastered dozens of spells that had been entirely out of the realm of my abilities only weeks before.

My mornings were spent in the castle, flitting around, behaving as if I were the useless ornament piece my father believed me to be. I got into the habit of sleeping late so that the mornings wouldn't seem so long.

Afternoons were my time. The moment Father left for his afternoon ride, I would slip away to my spell room and work until Alasdair came to inform me that Father had returned to the stables.

Everyone in my closest circle, save Father, knew of my work. Mary, Kip, Elspeth, Mae—each of them kept my secret.

Jerry's new position with my father provided him lodging and food, but most days he had little work to do. My father had little need of a messenger. If he wished to speak to anyone, Father preferred to meet face-to-face. So while Jerry's title offered him more esteem than the role of Kip's stable hand, most of his days were spent helping with the horses anyway. Each afternoon, he would allow me some time to work alone. Then later, he would stop in to check on my progress.

While my progress with magic was great, I'd found nothing in Grier's journals or spell books that ever mentioned time travel. I only had a few more books to work through, and I feared they would prove to be as fruitless as all the others.

"Yer hair is different."

Jerry's voice from behind caused me to jump. Even with my back toward him, I could sense that he stood close to me. I always tried to keep my distance from him. I didn't know how to handle the way my body stirred when near him.

Scooting to the side to clear him, I turned.

"Ye scared me. Aye, the wetness of the basement makes it grow to twice its normal width. Mary said if I continue to arrive to dinner appearing so disheveled, Father will begin to suspect that something is awry. I doona believe she's right. Father would have to look at me for more than the span of one breath to notice, but I suppose 'tis best to be safe." Stepping even further away, I continued, "Ye are earlier than usual. Does Kip not need ye?"

Grunting, Jerry rolled his eyes as he shook his head.

"I think I angered him. He's no older than I, but he is as impatient as a crotchety, old man. He knows everything I told him was true, but he dinna wish to hear it."

With both hands against my makeshift stone desk, I hoisted myself so that I sat upon it. It wasn't the most ladylike position, but none of that ever seemed to matter in front of Jerry. I didn't know if it was the time he came from or simply his open personality, but I suspected I could appear before him in my shift without him balking at the sight of it.

"What did ye tell him?"

He smiled and stepped closer. I immediately regretted sitting down—now there was nowhere for me to escape to. Turning so that his back leaned against the table, he lifted himself and sat down so close that our fingers brushed. I swallowed and hoped he couldn't see my skin flush in the low light of the room.

"I canna tell ye. Not yet anyway. Once he calms down and sees the sense of what I suggested, I'll share the news with ye. So." He lifted a finger and pointed to the open book on my other side. "What have ye learned today?"

I dreaded disappointing him each and every day. Even though he always responded with patience and kindness, I knew his own fears that I might not be able to help him grew with each passing day.

Leaning over with my left hand, I closed the book.

"Nothing that will help ye, I'm afraid."

Keeping his smile steady, he locked eyes with me as he leaned across me, grabbing the book beneath my hand. His nose was so close it could've brushed against my cheek had he wished it. I held my breath so it wouldn't shake.

"'Tis not what I asked. Sometimes, I believe ye think all I care about is ye helping me. 'Tis untrue. I believe I want ye to learn everything ye can about magic just as much as yer brother does. I would support anything that would give ye power over yer father's grip on ye, Morna. I'm genuinely interested. What did ye learn?"

I reached over to thumb the book open to the page I'd been working on as Jerry braced the book with his hands.

"'Tis a truth potion. Mary is gathering the necessary herbs. Would ye like me to try it on ye?"

Jerry jumped off the table so quickly he created a breeze. Laughing, he backed away and held up his hands as if to block me.

"Please doona ever slip me a potion. While I know I must use magic to get home, I've truthfully a great fear of it."

"Of magic?"

Such a confession surprised me. If he was afraid of magic, why did he come to my spell room each and every day and expose himself to it? Why had he lived with a witch far more powerful than me for over a year?

"Not of magic, per say, but of being controlled by it."

"Do ye truly believe I would do that to ye?"

His features softened.

"No, I doona believe ye would."

Slowly, he closed the distance between us, and I held my breath as his thighs bumped into my knees as he stood in front of me. Leaning in, he whispered, "Hold still, lass. Ye've a lash that is perilously close to falling into yer eye."

If not for my hands steadying me against the table, I would've trembled at the touch of his fingers across my lashes. With a soft pinch, he grabbed at something but blew it away before I could see the lash in his palm.

He stepped away as quickly as he neared me, and I held his eyes until he turned away. I could only see the shape of his eyes—the corner of the room where I sat was far too dark for him to see any of my lashes.

He said nothing else as he left.

I sat smiling long after he'd gone.

He had no real reason to touch me at all.

Jerry

For over a year, getting back to my own time was my greatest obsession. Every minute of every day, it was all I thought about. Even in my dreams, all I could see was my home. How could I relinquish my obsession so easily? Was any lass that powerful?

She couldn't see it yet—how much I cared for her. Her innocence prevented her from seeing how desperately I wanted her. I was thankful for it. For if Morna ever reciprocated my feelings, I wasn't sure I would ever be able to make myself leave this time, even if she found a way for me to return home.

And I had to return home. Of course I did. If my destiny lay in this time, I would've been born here.

Regardless, each day when I snuck down into Morna's basement, I hoped her news would be the same as the day before. Despite my better judgment, I hoped she found nothing.

It couldn't last forever. Either she would have to find the spell soon, or my willpower would betray me completely.

One way or another, I had to return. And no matter how much I wished it, I couldn't bring Morna with me.

It was torture to be near her, but it drove me mad to be away from her, even for the length of one morning.

Life at Conall Castle was miserable.

I was the happiest I'd ever been.

Chapter 15

"Psst…"

It was only mid-morning, still too early for Father to leave on his ride. So I sat in the garden watching Elspeth prune her beloved flowers as I heard the noise for the second time.

"Psst..."

Turning to look for the source of the noise, I found Jerry peeking around one of the garden's tallest bushes. He waved me toward him with one finger while he quietly called to me.

"Come here, lass. I wish to show ye something. Ye willna wish to miss it."

Making my excuses to Elspeth, I hurried after him. He latched onto my hand and quickly pulled me away from the garden the moment I reached him.

"What is it? Why are we running?"

I lifted my dress with my free hand so I could keep up with him. We ran together all the way to the small woods just opposite Kip's stables. Jerry said nothing until he pulled up short behind a wide tree.

"It may take a few moments, but we canna miss it. Lean over and watch, but doona let Kip see ye. He willna do it if he knows he's being watched."

My curiosity was piqued. I lay my hands against the tree trunk for support and leaned far over to my left. All I could see was the side of the stables.

"What am I watching for?"

I stilled as Jerry's hands touched the trunk on either side of my waist. He leaned forward, his front pressed against my back, his cheek just a hair's width from my own as he waited and watched with me.

"Ye'll know the moment ye see it, I'm certain."

It seemed as if days passed before Kip left the stable and moved where we could see him. All the while Jerry remained with his arms around me. I was so aware of his breathing that I didn't notice how my own had escalated until I glanced down to see my bosom rise and fall with humiliating speed. Inhaling deeply, I tried to forget about how it felt to have Jerry so close and focus on the scene in front of me.

Kip paced the length of the stable, muttering something to himself that neither of us could hear. After three full lengths of pacing, I saw Mary approaching, and my heart nearly stopped.

"Do ye mean? Does Kip mean to?"

Lifting his left arm from the tree's trunk, Jerry placed his finger against my lips to silence me. The warmth of his breath against my neck caused me to shiver all over.

"Shh lass, just watch."

Mary looked shocked to find Kip standing outside the stables, but it didn't take long for her to fall into conversation with him.

I watched with joy as Kip fidgeted nervously from foot to foot. I was certain he wasn't hearing a word Mary was saying—he was too busy trying to gather his courage.

She didn't realize what he meant to do at first. Even as Kip reached for her hands, Mary continued to chatter away as if nothing were odd about his behavior.

The moment she realized what Kip was doing, her hands flew to her mouth and she started to cry.

Even unable to hear the words that passed between them, I knew her answer by the way her arms flew around his neck.

The moment they kissed, I turned away, not wanting to intrude on their private moment. Unthinking, I turned right into Jerry's wide arms.

I couldn't move without touching him, and he didn't pull away as I stood with my nose level with his chin.

Desperate to decrease the tension between us, I began to chatter away incessantly.

"Thank ye for bringing me here. I canna believe Kip finally gathered the courage. Mary will be so happy. They're suited nicely, I think. I..."

His breath still warm against my ear, Jerry spoke. "Hush, lash. They're still here. Do ye wish for us to be found out?"

Why didn't he step away? I hated how nervous I felt in front of him.

I responded in a whisper. "No, o'course I doona. Is this what ye spoke to Kip about?"

He nodded. "Aye."

"I wouldna have thought ye a romantic, Jerry."

He leaned back just far enough so that he could look down at me. His eyes lingered on my lips. I desperately wanted to duck and move away from him.

Just as I was about to run, he pulled away.

"They're gone now. I've a heart for romance when it comes to others. I've no interest in it myself."

I knew little of love, but I knew every word Jerry said was a lie. If my own discomfort hadn't been so evident, I had no doubt Jerry would've kissed me.

"Is that so? Do ye not worry that ye will be lonely?"

His voice was colder than usual when he spoke. The intimacy between us only moments ago was gone, and that Jerry was now replaced with someone distant and dismissive.

"Do ye believe marriage means ye willna be lonely? I've known many who were far more lonely once married than they ever were before."

Although I found the notion depressing, I suspected it to be true.

"Mayhap so. Did ye know I've another suitor arriving tomorrow?"

His brows lifted in surprise. The thought of another man coming here with the intent to marry me bothered him. His jaw clenched and his hands bunched into fists as soon as I told him. His actions and words were at complete odds with one another.

"Why are ye telling me that? I doona believe yer father will wish me to dine with all of ye again. Even as much as he likes me, now that I am castle staff, there is no place for me at the table."

"I only thought ye should know so that ye willna be surprised if I doona have as much time to devote to my magic."

112

Huffing, Jerry turned and began the walk back to the castle.

"Lass, I'd wager ye will spend more time in yer basement once he arrives. This fool will bore ye just as much as the last."

I hurried to follow after him.

"Why would ye say that? Ye doona know him."

"I doona need to know him. I know ye. Any lad yer father picks willna suit ye."

I was inclined to agree with him.

"Jerry, if I dinna know any better, I'd say ye were jealous of me spending time with someone other than ye."

Keeping his back toward me, he increased his speed.

"'Tis good that ye know better then. I'll not be coming to the spell room today. Let me know if ye find anything."

Grinning, I went in search of Mary to congratulate her.

Whether he realized it or not, Jerry was definitely jealous.

Chapter 16

"**D**o ye think ye'll marry this one?"

I choked on my laughter as Mary yanked roughly at the laces on the back of my dress.

"Doona tie them so tightly, Mary. No, I know I willna marry this one. I've no desire for this lad to want me. Can ye pull my hair up so that it looks rather dreadful?"

Slipping her fingers beneath the laces, she pulled them loose.

"Ye are daft if ye think ye've any hope of dissuading him with the way ye pin yer hair. Did ye not see the way he looked at ye when he arrived?"

Shrugging, I faced her as she finished the laces.

"I suppose most would find him rather attractive, aye?"

Mary snorted and her cheeks flushed red.

"Do ye mean to say that ye doona find him handsome? Why, if not for Kip's recent proposal, I would happily tup him. Though, I'd have to fill my ears with cotton before letting him near me. The sound of his voice makes me want to weep."

Laughing until my sides hurt, I nodded in agreement. Mary didn't speak like any other lady I'd ever known. I loved her for it. And she wasn't wrong about Seumas McCabe's voice. He

115

spoke through his nose, making every word sound breathy and thick. It made him sound ill, even though he looked anything but.

Objectively, I could see that most would find him handsome. He wasn't tall like the men in my family, but he was astonishingly muscular with long blond hair and eyes so blue they were almost white.

"I find him difficult to look at, Mary. I doona wish to sit near him at dinner. How then am I meant to get to know him?"

Astonished, Mary twisted her head to the side as she eyed me skeptically.

"Ye canna look at him? I can hardly keep from doing so."

I shivered as I moved so Mary could fix my hair.

"'Tis his eyes, I think. They unsettle me. While I've thankfully never seen a fairy, I imagine they would look much like him, only a wee bit smaller."

Chuckling, Mary combed through my mess of curls.

"I've never thought of it myself, but aye, his eyes are verra different. Does yer father like him?"

"Aye, Father's known him for a decade. He's at least fifteen years older than me, ye know. He's already laird of his own territory."

"He doesna look fifteen years older than ye. Alasdair willna like him."

Alasdair didn't like him. I already knew that with certainty. While this morning was the first time I'd met Seumas McCabe, he and Alasdair shared a history. After Grier and some time before Elspeth entered my brother's life, both men had fallen for the same woman.

116

It surprised me that Mary didn't know the story of what had happened between them, but I was curious as to why she assumed my brother wouldn't like him.

"Why do ye say that?"

"Morna, if Seumas looks at ye in front of Alasdair the way he looked at ye when he arrived here, I'm afraid yer brother might try to strangle him in the middle of the meal."

"'Twould at least provide wee Eoin some amusement during what is certain to be a miserably long evening."

Satisfied that my hair didn't look its best, I stood, thanked Mary, and made my way down to dinner.

Perhaps in candlelight, I wouldn't find his eyes so startling.

Alasdair didn't lunge across the table, but each time Seumas touched my arm or brushed my shoulder, he looked as if he wanted to. His face would redden, his teeth would clench, and I would watch as Elspeth quietly reached over to squeeze his hand to calm him.

It was a tense evening, but my father remained oblivious to all of it. Always an expert at conversation, he visited and laughed and seemed quite pleased with himself over his choice of suitor. When at last the meal came to an end, I stood to bid Seumas farewell, only to be stopped by Father's voice at the end of the table.

"Mayhap, ye should show Seumas Elspeth's garden?"

Before I even had a chance to glance in Aladair's direction for help, my brother stood and nudged Elspeth to do the same.

"Aye, why doona we all take a turn outdoors? 'Tis a pleasant enough evening for it."

Grateful that I wouldn't be forced to walk with Seumas alone, I took his arm as he offered it to me and followed my brother and Elspeth out into the garden.

It was a rare and beautiful Scottish evening. The air was unusually warm, and it caused all the wonderful smells from Elspeth's flowers and plants to surround us. While I did my best to stay close to Alasdair, Seumas' strength demanded that we follow the pace he set, and I watched with dread as Elsepeth and Alasdair slowly disappeared around the corner in front of us.

Once alone, I would be forced to talk to him. I didn't wish to hear his voice for anything, but as we walked down one of the garden's pathways, the silence quickly became unbearable.

"'Tis a lovely night. Yer home is north, aye? Do ye ever have evenings as warm as this?"

I looked up to see him staring down at me. Mary was right. A hunger lay in his eyes that caused my stomach to clench uncomfortably.

"Aye, 'tis north and aye, at times we've as lovely weather as ye do. I can assure ye, ye'll be quite comfortable there."

His assumption made me feel suddenly defiant, and I pulled away to face him.

"Ye seem quite certain of yerself. Ye do know that Father has agreed to let me make this choice on my own, aye?"

He nodded and smiled, and I had to resist the urge to shiver. Such unearned confidence reminded me of my father. It made me like him even less.

"Aye, he told me. 'Tis not a concern. Do ye know how many lassies would sell their soul to be where ye are, lass—to

118

have the opportunity to marry me? I doona doubt ye'll come to see that ye willna have a better offer."

Clearing my throat, I walked past him and back toward the castle. I would tell Father come morning that Seumas could leave.

"Goodnight, Laird McCabe. Thank ye for the walk."

Before I could distance myself from him, his strong hand gripped my arm.

"I'll walk ye back to the castle."

I tried to pull away, but he held me too tightly.

"'Tis unnecessary, truly. I know my way around these grounds well."

"I'll sleep better, lass, knowing I saw ye safely inside."

I didn't believe Seumas was worried about my safety for a moment, but I allowed him to escort me toward the castle. A lifetime of living with my father made me practiced in appeasing boorish men. Often it was simply easier to allow them to believe they'd won.

Just outside the main doors, Seumas stopped, pushing me so that my back met with stone as he leaned in close.

"I'd like to kiss ye, lass. I'm certain 'twould do much to make ye want to marry me."

I would've laughed at him had his face not been so perilously close to my own. I couldn't risk the movement for fear it would cause my mouth to brush his.

As I lifted my palms to push him away, a shadow in the distance caught my eye. Standing far away, watching us, was Jerry. Suddenly all I could think about was just how much my kissing Seumas would displease him. It made me want to kiss the man all night long.

"Lass, did ye hear me? I'd like to kiss ye. Will ye allow it?"

Seumas' lips grazed my ear as he spoke, and I shivered as I pulled my gaze away from Jerry.

I reached my hands to the sides of Seumas' face and pulled his mouth to mine.

Chapter 17

I took four steps inside the castle before a small but strong hand reached out from the darkness and pulled me toward the kitchen.

"Mary, what are ye doing? I've had enough people grabbing me this evening."

Bending over from laughter, Mary continued to drag me down the stairs.

Still rattled from Seumas' wandering tongue, I was too dazed to fight her. As we entered the kitchen, she reached for a small, wooden stool and quickly saw me seated.

"Are ye all right, Morna? I feared ye might suffocate beneath his lips. If not for ye pulling away from him when ye did, I intended to charge ye to break his grip on ye."

Wiping my mouth with the back of my hand, my face warmed in embarrassment as I looked at her.

"Ye watched us? Was everyone in the whole castle watching?"

She smiled and hugged her waist as she laughed again.

"Ye best hope yer brother dinna see it, but aye, I did. I'm glad, too. Now, I'll be able to sleep without dreaming of the fool. Seeing the way he kissed ye cured me of any fantasies I possessed of him."

I couldn't see the humor in any of it.

"So, 'tis not always so bad then?"

"Lass, that was no kiss. Are ye sure he dinna have a twig and some chalk in his mouth? It looked as if he meant to clean yer teeth."

Relief washed over me in such a warm wave that before I could respond, I bent over and lost myself in a fit of laughter that rivaled Mary's. As long as Seumas' kiss wasn't what I would have to become accustomed to over a lifetime, I imagined I would recover.

"'Twas terrible, Mary. I doona think I even kissed him back. He dinna give me the chance."

Patting my shoulder with one hand, Mary reached up to tidy my hair with her other.

"Oh, I know, lass. It tired me to watch it. Ye best get to bed and rest. I only wanted to make certain ye were all right."

"Thank ye, Mary."

"I'll walk with ye to yer room just in case Seumas dinna go to his own bedchamber right away."

Climbing up the stairs together, we both peeked around the corners to make certain Seumas was no longer roaming around the castle. Finding the halls empty, we walked quietly to the end of the hall where my beloved bedchamber lay. I didn't know if I'd ever been so ready to hide within its walls.

My hands were at the laces on the back of my dress even before the door shut behind Mary. I was desperate to get out of my dress and into something I could breathe in. As I pulled the bottom bow loose, a hand covered my own. As I tried to scream, another hand covered my mouth.

Warm breath traveled down the length of my neck.

"As tempted as I am to let ye keep undressing, I know ye'd never forgive me if I did. Wait to undo yer laces until I leave."

Every limb of my body went limp as I recognized Jerry's voice. If not for his arms steadying me from behind, I would've fallen. I was safe. Jerry would never hurt me.

The relief of knowing it was him inside my room comforted me for only the briefest of moments before rage took hold.

As he removed his hand from my mouth, I turned and shoved him as hard as I could.

"What are ye doing? Ye scared me to death, Jerry."

"What am I doing? What the bloody hell do ye think ye were doing?"

It was the closest thing to yelling I'd ever heard come from Jerry's mouth. It was only then that I saw just how angry he really was. The muscles in his jaw bulged from clenched teeth, and his nostrils flared with every breath. He seemed to be vibrating with anger.

I'd allowed Seumas to kiss me in the hope that it would upset him, but I'd never expected it to anger him. At most, I thought it would annoy him.

"Do ye mean my kiss with Seumas?" I tried not to look disgusted as I thought back on it. "I doona think 'tis any of yer concern."

He growled as he stomped closer to me. I took a step back for every step he took forward. With Jerry more than anyone, I found distance to be important for my sanity.

"'Tis my concern when a lass as beautiful and infuriating as ye goes and wastes her verra first kiss on a bloke that wouldna know how to kiss ye properly if he spent his whole life learning to do so, just to anger me."

Every word startled me. Jerry thought me beautiful. My kiss had angered him. How did he know it had been my first kiss?

I couldn't let Jerry see how much power his words had over me—just how much his nearness caused me to shake. I crossed my arms and attempted to lean casually against the stone window ledge at my back.

"What makes ye believe 'twas my first kiss?"

He laughed slightly as he stepped toward me. Once again with him, I no longer had anywhere to go.

"Lass, do ye think me daft? Yer Father keeps watch on everything ye do. We have to hide ye away so ye might practice magic. When in yer life would ye have had the opportunity to sneak away to kiss men in the village? And I know already that ye rarely have visitors here. Yer suitors are the first in a verra long time. Ye've had no opportunity to kiss anyone. And now, the first chance ye've had in all yer life to do so, ye waste it on that ignorant arse."

"I dinna waste it. 'Twas a lovely kiss."

Jerry's jaw clenched again, and I repressed a smile as I thought of how attractive I found him when angry. It was different than Father's anger. Jerry kept it controlled, and he wasn't angry for the sake of being angry. He was angry because he actually felt things deeply.

"Lying doesna suit ye, Morna. Ye hated every minute Seumas' hands were on ye."

Enjoying myself more than was truly proper or kind, I continued to deny his claims.

"'Tis no lie. 'Tis possible I'll end up marrying Seumas."

Jerry now stood inches away. His voice shook as he spoke. His eyes were locked with my lips.

"Is that so, lass? Ye think ye will marry him?"

My breathing escalated as I watched Jerry's expression. There was a need in it that I'd never seen before. Unlike Seumas' gaze, having Jerry want me warmed me through.

"Aye." My own voice came out on a breath, so soft that he wouldn't have been able to hear me if not for his nearness. "Mayhap, I will."

His hands lifted to my face, and I gasped at the touch of his palms against my skin. Brushing against the apples of my cheeks with his thumbs, Jerry leaned in until our noses touched.

"If 'tis true lass, I'll be damned if I let ye marry another man without ever experiencing a proper kiss."

His lips were warm and soft, and he kissed me with a gentleness that caused every sense within me to stir. I wasn't a passive partner in this kiss. We gave and took in equal measure. With each breath, our familiarity with one another grew.

He smiled against me, and slowly his tongue grazed my lips as I trembled beneath him. One hand at the small of my back pulled me closer. As my front pressed against him, his hands moved to my hair.

Jerry kissed me until every thought in my mind was of him. Every time he tried to pull away, I held him close. I'd never felt anything so intensely in my life.

"Lass." The touch of his lips against my neck caused me to moan. "Lass, I must go. 'Tis

a blessing I had ye retie yer laces. I wouldna be able to leave had ye undressed. Please doona ever let that man kiss ye again. I doona think I can bear it."

He turned without another word, leaving me shaking and wanting in a way entirely new and unfamiliar to me.

125

Everything seemed different now. I was finally truly awake for the first time in my life.

Chapter 18

Jerry

I cursed myself every step of the way back toward my new home in the castle's outer cottage. I would feel her lips against mine every day until I died, but I couldn't allow my own selfishness to ruin the sweet lassie's life, and it very well could if I wasn't careful.

While I tried to cling to my desire to return home to my own time, it lessened every day. And what did that mean for me? What did it mean for her? If I stayed here, what life could I give her? Nothing like the life she deserved. Nothing like the life to which she was accustomed. If her desire for me half matched my own, there was only one thing I could do to correct what had passed between us.

I would have to break her heart and keep my distance until I could return to the time from which I came.

Morna

Ididn't sleep at all after Jerry left. I spent the night lying blissfully awake, and when morning came, I felt rested and well. All I wanted to do was see him again.

I took extra time and care readying myself for the day. When I left my room mid-morning, I nearly retreated back inside as I saw Seumas standing at the end of the hall. But he saw me before I could escape so I was forced to approach him.

"Good morning, lass. Ye look beautiful. Are ye ready to tell yer father of our plans to wed?"

He offered me his arm, but I refused it. He would have to be told eventually. Now would have to do.

"I am sorry if I misled ye, but I willna marry ye. I doona think we suit each other. I know ye traveled far, and I doona doubt that Father will allow ye to stay here as long as ye wish to prepare for your journey home, but ye willna leave here betrothed to me."

I wouldn't have thought it possible for his already shockingly pale face to lose any more color, but it did. He stepped back as if I'd slapped him.

"I'll give ye the day to change yer mind. Only a fool would refuse me."

He was so much like my father. It was so impossible for him to see or relate to how anyone else might feel.

"I doona need another day, Seumas. I'm a fool."

I left him balking as I went in search of the man I really wanted to marry.

I found Jerry in the stables, stroking Father's horse, with Kip nowhere to be found.

He looked different than he had the night before. The warm glow inside me dulled as I neared him. He grew rigid as I walked the length of the stables, and he didn't smile as he looked at me.

Jerry smiled at everyone.

"Titus is a good horse. He deserves a better rider than Father."

Huffing, Jerry turned away and continued to run his hands down Titus' neck.

"I canna disagree with ye, though I believe the horse to be rather fond of him. Animals are devoted creatures. Their hearts are so much more pure."

I didn't know what I'd intended by coming to the stables. I just wanted to see him, to feel his lips against my own once again.

"Do ye enjoy the stable work? Ye wouldna have to do it, ye know? 'Tis not what Father requires of ye."

He moved to the other side of the horse. I couldn't reconcile the feeling of intimacy between us the night before with how the distance between us felt now. It was as if Jerry had built a wall of stone up between us.

"I prefer it. 'Tis possible ye could find the spell I need while I'm away for yer father, and I doona wish for that to happen. As soon as ye find the spell, I must leave here."

I don't know why it hadn't occurred to me—why his kiss had so completely obliterated all thought of Jerry leaving from my mind—but it had.

"Ye…ye still wish to leave then?"

He glanced up, locked eyes with me, and laughed.

"Aye, o'course. Ye dinna think…ye dinna think that last night changed anything, did ye, lass?"

He paused, and a bone-chilling pain swept through my body. I watched in horror as he continued, shattering something deep inside me with every new word.

"Doona feel badly if ye did, lass. 'Tis my own fault. 'Tis easy to forget when looking at ye just how young and ignorant ye are."

Despite the sudden deep ache in my chest, my pride wouldn't allow me to fall apart in front of him. If he meant to make me feel foolish, I wouldn't allow it. Inexperienced as I was, I knew he cared for me.

Opening the door to Titus' stall, I moved to corner Jerry. Smiling, I leaned in close to him. He didn't move away, and I didn't miss how his breath caught as I reached out to touch his chest.

"Do ye think ye are the only one with the ability to tell when someone is lying, Jerry? While ye may verra well return home when I find what we need to get ye there, there is no sense in pretending things are no different between us now. Aye, I am young, which is no fault of my own, but I am not ignorant. Doona be an arse, or I'll never let ye kiss these lips again. Do ye understand me?"

I didn't back away as I watched him. Slowly, as his breathing quickened, the iciness in his gaze fell way to one of hunger. I readied myself for his touch only to feel a sudden breeze as he stepped away at the sound of footsteps. From the other end of the stables, my brother's voice called to us.

"Jerry, Morna, are ye in here? I looked in the spell room and even asked Mary where ye might be. I need to speak with ye."

I remained in the stall with Titus as Jerry went out to meet my brother, and I hurriedly tried to calm my own breathing. Alasdair permitted Jerry and I to be alone together only because it had never crossed his mind that there was anything other than friendship between us. He could suspect nothing if either of us wanted to be allowed to continue our afternoons in my spell room.

"Aye, Morna is in with Titus. What is it?"

Leaning around Titus' large back end, I smiled and raised a hand in greeting to my brother as he called to me.

"Come here, lass. Anything that has to do with magic we must discuss where none can hear."

Once I made my way out into the center of the stables to stand with them, my brother excitedly gave us his news.

"I've heard news of a clan—they lay so far north that I could find none that have ever actually met them—but stories of their druid have traveled throughout Scotland for decades. I've learned that this man is known to train those with magic. I believe we should go in search of him. Surely, if he was to see what natural power ye possess, he would help ye."

I would gladly take any teaching I could get, but there was no way Father would allow me to leave here, and Alasdair would never leave Elspeth and Eoin for such a long journey. Only one of us could go—Jerry.

Without hesitation, Jerry began to ready a horse, questioning my brother as he did so.

"Aye, o'course we should find him. Do ye know precisely where they lay? I've traveled most of Scotland and have never heard of such a clan."

Pulling a piece of weathered parchment from the waist of his kilt, Alasdair extended it toward Jerry. I watched as he stared at it intensely for a long moment.

"'Twill take me months to travel there and back. We best all hope that such a long journey is successful."

Alasdair nodded, and panic rose inside me. Everything was happening too fast. Jerry couldn't leave. Not now. Not for two months or more.

"Is there such urgency that ye must leave now? Should we not discuss it further?"

"Discuss what, lass? Ye know as well as I, ye've only a few of Grier's journals left. If ye canna find the spell on yer own, we must get help."

Alasdair interrupted, and I struggled to hold back tears.

"Doona worry about Father, Jerry. I'll make an excuse for ye that he willna question. Be careful and return to us as quickly as ye can."

Desperate to have him stay, I ran to the horse as he mounted, grabbing onto his leg.

"What will ye do for food? Ye should at least wait to have Mary prepare provisions for ye."

He smiled and leaned down to rest his hand on my shoulder.

"I survived for months without Mary's meals. I shall be fine."

Bending so that Alasdair couldn't hear him, he whispered, "Lass, if ye care at all for Seumas, marry him, for I canna promise ye that I will return. Should this druid have the means to send me home, I shall beg him to do it, and then I will send him to ye to train ye. If more than two months pass without my return, doona expect to see me again."

I thought I saw tears fill his eyes, but he tore quickly away from me, nudging his horse as he called a farewell to Alasdair.

The moment both Jerry and Alasdair were gone from the stables, I dropped to the floor and wept.

Chapter 19

Father found me crying in Elspeth's garden after returning from his daily ride. I didn't visit my spell room after Jerry left, and I spent the rest of the day avoiding everyone, content to wallow in my own self-pity.

How could he leave so easily? And his words made it plain enough that he had no intention of returning here. The sudden nature of his departure reminded me so much of Grier's banishment that old feelings of loss and abandonment dredged their way up, leaving me totally miserable.

Father joined me on the ground next to the roses without a word. Unable to acknowledge his own emotions about anything, he hadn't any idea how to deal with emotions that didn't belong to him.

Uncomfortable with the silence, I brushed a tear from my eye and looked up at him.

"Do ye need something, Father? I'll not be good company for ye tonight."

In a show of affection so strange I had to resist the urge to pull away from him, Father took my hand and gathered it between his palms.

"I sent Seumas away, lass. He told me what he said to ye. Any man that doesna want ye is a fool."

The notion that Father believed my tears had anything to do with Seumas was more proof of how little he knew me.

"Doesna want me? What did he tell ye he said to me?"

Stroking my hand as if it were a kitten, Father looked down at it as he spoke.

"Ye needn't be embarrassed, Morna. Seumas' displeasure with ye has nothing to do with ye."

Pulling my hand away, I raised my voice in confusion. "Displeasure? What are ye talking about, Father?"

"Seumas came to me and said how he told ye this morning that he doesna wish to marry ye after meeting ye."

There was nothing I could say in my shock. Every new thing I learned about Seumas made him seem more like my father. His ego was so grand that rather than have anyone know he'd been rejected, he'd rushed to make others believe the choice had been his.

"Doona worry though, lass. I swore to him that I would never provide protection to his clan again. 'Tis his mistake, and he shall pay for it if ever he needs aid from a Conall."

I could tell no one of the real reason for my tears. So, as Father leaned awkwardly over to hug me, I allowed him to believe it had everything to do with Seumas.

"Alasdair has already sent word to Henry MacNeal. Do ye remember him? He and yer brother have always been good friends. 'Twas Alasdair who suggested the match. I never would have thought of it myself, but I believe ye may find him verra pleasing. He'll be here within a fortnight."

Two Weeks Later

My sadness remained as the weeks passed, and my attitude toward everyone in my life—the only exception being wee Eoin—turned to one of aggravation and hostility. As I stood at the castle's main entrance waiting to be introduced to yet another suitor, I was vibrating with irritation.

As Father left the rest of us standing inside, every bit of frustration I'd harbored toward my brother over the last two weeks exploded.

"I canna believe ye've joined him in this. Ye told me ye dinna see a need for it. Ye said I dinna need a husband until I wanted one. Now ye've gone and invited yer own choice here. It makes ye no better than him."

Looking to make certain Henry MacNeal and Father were still at the stables, Alasdair walked away, waving for me to follow. Once he entered the sitting room closest to us, he bent down to look at me at eye level.

"Is that what has been bothering ye all these days, Morna? Ye thought I'd betrayed my word to ye?"

Seeing the acknowledgement in my eyes, he stood and paced in front of me.

"Ye should have said something to me about this days ago, lass. I'd have happily explained everything to ye. I canna believe ye really thought I'd do such a thing."

"But ye did do such a thing." I couldn't withhold the venom in my voice.

"No, lass, I dinna. Do ye know who Father intended to invite here next?"

I shook my head and waited.

"Ludo Buchanan. Not only is the old fool thirty years older than ye, his temper is far worse than even Father's. I begged Father to allow me to pick the next suitor so ye wouldna be forced to be around him for a moment. I doona care if ye marry or not. If ye dislike Henry, ye can send him away just as ye've done the others, but at least I know he is a good man with no temper."

I allowed my brother's words to sink in as the anger inside me dissipated for the first time in days.

Apologizing for my behavior, I moved to wrap my arms around him.

"I should've known. There is a good reason for everything ye do. Thank ye."

Squeezing me tight, Alasdair slowly pulled away and began to lead me back to where Elspeth and Eoin stood waiting.

"I love ye, Morna. I'll always protect ye. Now, doona greet Henry with the same callousness ye've shown all of us lately. At least give the lad a chance. Ye'll like him."

I turned and stilled.

The second my eyes locked with Henry's, I knew Alasdair was right.

I would like him very much.

Chapter 20

Note from M.C.

Perhaps there were signs I should've seen, but I've long since forgiven myself for not. I was too young, too sheltered, too desperate to find my way to have made any better decisions than I did. If there is one amongst us that isn't at some point fooled by the charms of another, I've yet to meet them.

None of what happened in the months following Henry's arrival was Alasdair's fault. He couldn't possibly have known. Regardless, I know my brother carried undue guilt for years.

His pain is the only thing in my past I would change—my brother deserved more happiness than anyone I've ever known. Yet his life saw him bear so much sorrow.

And so much of it was entirely my fault.

One Month Later

I watched Elspeth carefully as we readied for the most exciting event to happen in Conall territory since Elspeth and Alasdair's wedding years earlier—the impending marriage of Kip and Mary.

Elspeth's skin was glowing, but the vibrancy of her skin didn't match her behavior at all. She was so exhausted she could barely summon the strength to dress.

I'd only seen her behave in such a way once before.

"Have ye told Alasdair, yet?"

Flippantly, she glanced over her shoulder at me.

"Told him what?"

Smiling, I walked over and placed my hands on her shoulders.

"That ye are with child again. Ye are, aye?"

Spinning to face me, she grabbed my hands in a plea and stood.

"Oh, ye canna tell him, Morna, not yet. I've lost babes before, and I doona wish to put Alasdair through it again. I will say nothing to him until I can no longer hide it."

"O'course." I understood Elspeth's concern. While every miscarriage broke her heart, Alasdair took it even harder. It wasn't only his own grief that he felt—he felt Elspeth's pain just as acutely. He was always trying to carry everyone else's heartache.

I watched as she allowed herself to smile, and I leaned forward to hug her.

"Ye feel different about this one though, aye? I can see in yer eyes that ye are not as worried."

Her chin rested against my shoulder as she spoke.

"Aye, I doona know why, but I feel stronger than in the past."

She paused as she broke away from me and looked out the window. Motioning with her head, she urged me to look.

"Does he look angry to ye, as well?"

Down below, Henry stood with one of his men, his expression different from any I'd ever seen on him before. His face was red. While we could hear nothing, he was most certainly screaming at the poor man standing across from him.

"Aye, verra angry. What do ye suppose the lad did to deserve it?"

Elspeth reached to grab my hand in the motherly way that came so naturally to her.

"The fact that ye believe any one that serves ye deserves to be yelled at rather than spoken to says much about the man who raised ye. Ye know as well as I do, Alasdair would never speak to anyone in such a way. My own father never raised his voice in all his life."

Elspeth's sudden passion on the subject surprised me. She'd read much more into the scene than I had.

"I think ye are assuming much from what we just saw, Elspeth. I've often been known to yell at people. So have ye from time to time."

"'Tis different when we yell at those we love. 'Tis love that incites our passion towards anger or disagreement. When a man yells at those who serve him—when they are not a friend or loved one—there is no passion in that, only cowardice."

Too curious to let her words lay, I pressed further as I reached the doorway.

"Are ye trying to tell me something, Elspeth?"

"Only that ye should pay close attention to everything Henry does. Take note of his habits, his words, his glances. Ye need to know someone well before ye agree to spend yer life with them."

I enjoyed Henry's company immensely. His friendship and the distraction his company provided were all that kept me from wallowing in my anger at Jerry every waking moment.

"I doona plan to marry him. I consider him a friend. I must ready myself. I'll see ye downstairs shortly."

As I stepped into the hallway, I thought I heard Elspeth say, "Ye are not his friend, ye are his target," but I couldn't be sure.

Mary and Kip's wedding was beautiful. Kip cried—something I would've never imagined possible—and Mary looked radiant and happy standing next to her new husband.

It was a perfect day, but I couldn't see Mary and Kip together without thinking of Jerry and his part in their love story. Six weeks had passed since his departure, and only a fortnight remained until I would have to resign myself to the truth that I would never see him again.

"Where are ye, lass? For 'tis not here amongst the celebration."

There was no sign of the angry man I'd seen from Elspeth's window as I stirred in my seat and looked up into Henry's deep green eyes. His dimples showed as he smiled at me, and I happily took his arm as I stood.

"'Tis nothing. Did ye enjoy dancing with Mae? 'Twas kind of ye to indulge her cause."

With each passing day, Mae grew more determined in her quest to make Hew her husband. I expected that before long she would simply lose her patience and come right out and demand it of him. While Hew had of course been at the wedding to see his sister married, he'd done a splendid job of avoiding glancing in Mae's direction. Once the celebrations had begun, Mae made certain Hew was watching and then asked Henry to dance with her. And dance he had—with an abandon that managed to make even me jealous. I was certain their time together made Hew feel the same.

Henry smiled as he slowly led me away from the crowd.

"Aye, she's a lovely dancer. Each time I saw Hew look in our direction, I would pull the lass closer. He dinna care for it a bit."

I laughed as we walked away from the festivities and back toward the castle. No one would notice our absence. Alasdair and Elspeth were too busy visiting with everyone that passed them, and Father wouldn't return to the castle until he'd successfully danced with every lass in the village.

"Let us hope yer service will irritate him enough to inspire some courage. I doubt that it will though. He is the most painfully shy man I've ever met."

There was nothing shy about Henry. He could charm anyone with his kind manners. I'd never known anyone quite as talented at conversation. He made everyone he spoke with feel like they were the only person in the room.

"Aye, I feel rather sorry for him. Morna, lass, might I ask ye something?"

When we were far enough outside the village that none could see us, I allowed my head to rest against his arm as I moved in closer and wrapped my arm more tightly around his.

"O'course ye can."

"Do ye ever intend to allow me to kiss ye?"

His question took me aback. Henry was tediously proper and polite. I'd never picked up on any sign that he wished to kiss me. It was part of the reason I was so comfortable around him. He truly made me feel as if we were friends rather than suitors. More than once I'd wondered if perhaps Alasdair brought him here knowing he wouldn't wish to marry me just to buy me some time before the next suitor was forced to come here.

"Do ye have any desire to kiss me? I dinna think ye cared for me in that way."

He stopped and untwined my arm as he stepped back and held me at arm's length.

"Whatever made ye think I doona care for ye, lass? I've spent every moment of the past four weeks trying to convince ye that I do."

"'Tis only that we get on so well together. Ye've been so kind to me."

His brows creased together forming a deep line in his forehead.

"Are ye under the impression that if a man wishes to kiss ye he will be unkind to ye?"

I thought of Seumas' persistence and then of the anger that had inspired Jerry's kiss. Until his departure, I never would've considered Jerry to be unkind. Now, I couldn't think of him any other way.

"No, I dinna mean…" I faltered, not knowing what to say. "I thought ye wanted me only as yer friend. I thought perhaps 'tis what Alasdair instructed."

He looked even more baffled the more I spoke.

"Lass, Alasdair has instructed nothing. 'Twould do him little good if he tried to do so. I've treated ye as a friend because I feel ye are one, but that does not mean that I doona also wish to make ye my lover and my wife. 'Tis my own fault if I've allowed ye to believe differently. Allow me to rectify that now."

Henry's mouth was on mine in an instant, pulling me close as his mouth explored mine with a passion that caused me to moan involuntarily. There was nothing familiar in Henry's kiss, nothing that spoke to the friendship between us. As his hands roamed down my front, I realized for the first time what it meant to feel desire so strongly you would sacrifice just about anything to have it satisfied.

Henry kissed me until I could no longer hold myself up without the support of his hand at my back. As his free hand palmed my breast and my chest filled with heat, I knew I would never be able to think of him as my friend again.

Perhaps I'd been wrong before. Perhaps this was what love really was. Perhaps at the end of the next two weeks, I would be able to look at the passing date and simply say, *Jerry who?*

Chapter 21

Jerry

Even if I rode back from the Allen territory without stopping, I would never make it back to Conall Castle in a fortnight. The date loomed in my mind with a sense of dread comparable only to that I might have if it were the date of my own death. For in a way, if I returned to find Morna married to another, most especially to the utter fool Seumas McCabe, it would be.

I considered turning back at least a dozen times in the first days after leaving Conall territory. The stupidity of my words and the unnecessary harshness of them haunted me every night and day. What sort of madness had driven me to them? Desperation? Fear? A longing for her so deep I couldn't bear it?

Whatever the reason, I knew I couldn't turn back to apologize for them. For it wasn't only my own destiny that lay in the druid's hands, it was Morna's ability to unlock the power within her, as well. If I could find him and convince him to help her, everything would be worth it.

All of it had been for nothing.

147

The man I sought was not there, and no one within the territory had any inkling of when he might return. I couldn't wait. If I couldn't bring the druid back to her, I would at least return myself.

I swore to myself as I embarked on the long journey back that if Morna was unmarried when I arrived, I would never let her go again.

Morna

"So...how do ye feel? Different—now that ye're married?"

Only Mary could thaw my father's icy heart enough to convince him to allow her and Kip so many days away after their wedding. Alasdair arranged a lovely cabin for them a day's ride from the castle. So she and Kip had escaped to enjoy only each other for a full seven days after their wedding.

Upon her return to the castle, I awaited her in the kitchen. I'd missed her dreadfully.

"Oh, Morna." Mary patted the top of my head as if I were a child, smiling guiltily as she did so. "While ye will surely feel verra different after yer wedding night, I have never pretended to be the well-behaved lass ye are. I feel quite the same, only more sated and rested than I've been in years. 'Tis Kip who is a different man now. Poor lad was as innocent as a wee lamb."

Eyes wide with shock, I laughed and pulled out the stool next to me so she could sit.

"No? Do ye really mean it? Kip was a...a...he..." I was the innocent little lamb. I had so much more difficulty discussing such matters than Mary did.

"A virgin, lass. Aye, he was. I wouldna have believed it either, but the poor lad was terrified of me. Doona worry for him, though. I made certain he overcame his fear quickly enough."

I opened my mouth to ask her about their journey but stopped short when I noticed how she was watching me. Her arms were crossed and she had her head turned oddly to one side as she looked me over with just one eye.

"What is it? Is there something on me?"

She smiled, slow and wide. "Ye look different. Verra different. Is it possible ye and Henry have shared a similar experience as of late?"

Horrified at her implication, I nearly fell backwards out of my chair.

"No! O'course not. Whatever made ye think that?"

"Doona act so shocked, lass. Something happened whilst I was away. I can see by the way ye are bouncing in yer seat that ye wish to discuss it. Come on now. Out with it."

Consciously, it hadn't even been the reason why I'd gone to the kitchen, but I knew she was right. Mary was the only woman in my life with whom I could discuss absolutely anything. My mind was so muddled as of late, I feared I would grow mad from the confusion I constantly felt.

"Aye, fine. Can ye tell me why every man kisses so verra differently?"

Amused, Mary's smile remained as she scooted back in her seat and placed her hands on both my legs, effectively pinning me to my seat.

"Every man? I only know of the one ye've kissed. Have ye truly been so busy while I was away?"

"Only two others. Henry kissed me the night of yer wedding," I paused, realizing the dishonesty in my words, then finished, "and many times since. The other lad was some time ago."

Moving to cross her arms again, Mary stood and began walking in circles around the room. Mary was so used to spending every waking hour working that she could not sit still for more than a few brief moments.

"Ye canna mean Fulton, can ye? If that lad had the bravery to kiss ye, I shall be shocked. Even Hew is less shy than that poor bloke."

I'd spoken to no one of my conflicted feelings for Jerry, but it was killing me to keep them to myself.

"No, 'twas not Fulton. 'Twas Jerry."

"Ah."

She didn't look the least bit surprised.

"What do ye mean, 'ah?'"

"O'course 'twas Jerry. He's been in love with ye since the day ye found him."

My heart rallied against her words. I couldn't bear for them to be true. He wouldn't have left so easily if they were.

"No. Jerry used me in the hopes I could get him home. He doesna love me. The moment he learned of another who might be able to aid him more quickly, he left. He will never return here."

"Do ye truly believe that? 'Tis not why he left, lass. He left because his feelings frightened him. Men often run from such things. Ye doona have to believe me, but I'd wager two toes on the fact that he will return to ye. When he does, he will have realized just how foolish he was."

I couldn't spend my days hoping for his return. I thought about him enough as it was—even with the distraction Henry so willingly provided.

"Ye dinna answer my question, Mary."

She chuckled and leaned against the wall behind her.

"With the count ye've gathered over these past weeks, I'm not sure I have much more practice kissing men than ye do. Tell me what was so different about each man's kiss, and mayhap we can work through the *whys* of it together."

It amused Mary to see me so flustered over men. She was one of many who worried I would grow old alone.

"I hardly know what to say about Seumas' kiss."

Mary interrupted, laughter erupting between every word. "I saw that kiss with my own eyes. No need to say anymore. What of Jerry's kiss?"

Jerry's kiss repeated itself in my dreams. It seemed etched forever in some warm corner of my soul where all of my most precious memories remained.

"Jerry spoke to me with his kiss. 'Twas as if each touch of his lips was meant to tell me something—the way he held me stirred more than my body—it stirred something within my soul."

Mary's suspicious gaze was back. I cleared my throat in my haste to move on.

151

"I canna think when Henry kisses me. 'Tis as if I am consumed by him, and I disappear beneath his touch. I canna breathe nor think nor move, and I doona want to do anything other than keep kissing him when his hands are on me."

When I finished, Mary stood silently for a long time. I couldn't tell if when she spoke it would be through bursts of laughter or tears.

"Say something, Mary."

Eventually, she moved to sit next to me once again. Her voice was soft and serious when she spoke. "Have ye told Henry of yer magic?"

It had never occurred to me to tell him. "No."

"Why do ye think that is?"

I didn't know. I shrugged.

"When ye think of marrying Henry, how do ye feel?"

"I feel nothing. I doona ever think of marrying him."

She continued her inquisition as my head began to throb. "And why do ye think that is?"

Again, I shrugged.

"Lass, 'tis not a why, 'tis a whom."

His name slipped out before I could stop it. "Jerry."

"Aye. Ye already know the answer to yer own question, Morna. One man has awakened yer heart and soul, the other simply yer body. 'Tis up to ye to decide which ye desire more. Now, get out of my kitchen. The lassies who cared for it in my stead left it a fair mess."

Chapter 22

For the following fortnight, I allowed myself to ponder the possibility that Mary might be right about my feelings toward Henry and Jerry—that perhaps my feelings for Henry were based on nothing more than physical attraction, and it was Jerry who held my heart. If Jerry returned before the end of two months, I knew where my heart would lead me.

Two months to the day that Jerry left, I made my peace in the only way I knew how. I raged and cried and went to my spell room to search for a spell that might allow me to find him. Maybe he was on his way back. Maybe the druid hadn't been able to help him. Maybe something had slowed him down along the way. There were so many possibilities, and I couldn't bring myself to give up on him without trying to find out where he was.

I'd not entered the basement since Jerry left. In many ways, the room felt as if it were as much his as mine. He'd helped create it for me, and I could see every memory of us talking and laughing in my mind as if they were only yesterday. It still smelled of him, and it made the center of my chest ache dreadfully.

I knew the book I sought—one of the first I'd read. It detailed spells for visions that I had never naturally possessed.

I'd never had reason to try one of the spells until now. Such spells were tricky. So much depended upon the caster's intention—what lay in the mind of the witch as the spell was cast.

Grier's notes made it even more difficult to decide which one to use. There appeared to be multiple uses for each and every spell. I read for a long while and finally chose what I hoped would be the safest choice—a simple seer spell that was meant to show me the answer to whatever question was in my heart.

It was a simple recitation in Gaelic. As I put Jerry at the forefront of my mind, I recited the words with care. It was the strangest experience of my life. One moment, I could see the basement's stone wall in front of me, the next all I could see was a small home unlike any I'd seen before.

Its walls weren't stone, and its roof wasn't thatch. Through the window, the rooms appeared to be lit by hundreds of candles. Confused, I forced myself to glance around the scene. I gasped at the sight of a large wagon-like contraption I had no reference for.

Movement from within the home drew my attention back to the window. Tears filled my eyes as understanding sunk in. In the background, I could see a woman. Then as I continued to stare at the window, Jerry appeared, smiling widely as he reached to pull the draperies closed.

The scene confused me. It was the last thing I'd expected to see. Some desperate and hopeful part of my mind had been convinced I would find Jerry resting in the forest on his way back here. But he would never be back here again. Jerry had succeeded in finding his way home.

What I was seeing wasn't from my time, but his. The druid had helped him. Jerry was home, in his own time, happy with someone I could only assume was his wife. Oh, how she must have missed him while he was away for so long.

When the vision before me returned to my basement, I laid my head down and quietly cried myself to sleep.

It was dark when I woke. The candles had long since burned away. Feeling my way to the stairs, I climbed up out of my spell room to find the moon high in the sky. Many of the castle's windows were still lit with candlelight.

What excuse would I give when I entered the castle? Father would be furious, and Alasdair would be worried. Everyone would demand to know where I'd been.

As I rounded the corner, I spotted Mary, her short legs moving so quickly she was barely able to stop herself before smashing against me.

"Morna, ye must get inside. I've made excuses for ye as long as I can. Yer father was readying himself to go into the village to retrieve ye."

"Is that where he thought I was?"

Nodding, Mary grabbed my hand and pulled me along behind her.

"Aye, when ye dinna come to dinner, I told him ye'd left to help Mae."

"Why is he angry then? I often do go to help her."

Thank God for Mary. She'd thought of the only excuse he would believe.

"I doona know, lass. Ye've not done so since Henry arrived. I believe he thought it rude of ye to leave him. Doona worry. Just doona leave Henry's side once ye enter the castle. Yer father willna yell at ye in front of him."

Reaching to adjust my hair, I pulled at Mary's hand so she would slow down.

"How did ye know where I was?"

"I know what day it is, lass. I suspected ye might have escaped to yer spell room to spend the day alone."

Hugging me tight, Mary pulled away and pointed toward the castle. "Best get inside. Henry was in the sitting room with Alasdair when I last saw him."

Henry wasn't inside the sitting room when I entered. Neither was Alasdair. Only Father remained.

"Ah. Ye've decided to return. Come, lass. I wish to speak to ye."

"I'm sorry, Father. I wouldna have gone into the village unless I were truly needed."

Lies came too easily to me when speaking to Father.

He held up a hand to stop me. "'Tis not ye that I worry about. What will Mae do when ye leave here?"

"Leave? What do ye mean?"

Father motioned to the seat across from him. Almost every serious conversation I'd ever had with him had taken place in this room with us sitting opposite each other in just the same way.

"Doona be daft, lass. One way or another, 'tis time for ye to make a decision regarding Henry. He's shown far more patience with ye than I would have. Six weeks is a long time to make him wait."

"I doona think he's in any hurry, Father. He rarely speaks of it."

Father grunted and crossed his arms.

"As I said, the lad is patient. Ye care for him. I can see that ye do. Can ye think of one reason ye shouldna marry him?"

My only reason was now living centuries ahead of me.

"One day I may wish to marry him. I am not ready to leave here yet. I wish to see wee Eoin grow."

I said nothing of the new babe. While Elspeth would be forced to tell Alasdair soon, news of the babe was still our secret.

"Morna." Father's voice was stern, cold, distant. "Eoin will grow up fine without ye. 'Tis generous of me to allow ye to pick yer husband at all. 'Tis not up to ye to decide how long ye reside in my home."

I rarely allowed Father's words to hurt me, but with my heart still sore from learning Jerry truly had returned home, the protective wall I normally kept up between me and my father crumbled.

It was natural for daughters to marry and leave their father's home. I only wanted him to be more saddened at the thought of me leaving. Even if I wasn't truly his, had our years together not bonded him to me in some way that made him love me?

"Are ye so eager to see me gone from here? Will ye not miss me at all?"

Father's eyes softened in the same way they always did when he played with Eoin.

"O'course I'll miss ye." He paused and sighed then opened his arms and waved me toward him. "Come and sit on my knee."

I stared back at him blankly. Never in my life had my father held me. Slowly, I stood and walked toward him and lowered myself onto his lap. It felt strange and foreign, and for some reason I couldn't explain, it made me want to cry.

"I've not always treated ye as I should. I know ye wonder if I care for ye as I do Alasdair. I do, lass. I love ye so much it pains me. Do ye know how much ye remind me of yer mother? Every time I look at ye, I see her. As similar as ye are in personality, I canna believe that ye never knew her.

"No matter how things ended between us, yer mother was the love of my life. If I've distanced myself from ye, 'tis only to prevent the pain I feel when I see her reflected in ye. Ye must wed not because I doona want ye here, but because I must ensure that ye will always be cared for—even after I'm gone."

I couldn't imagine a world without him. I feared so many things about my future, but losing my father had never been one of them. He was so strong, so forceful. Although I knew it foolish, it was truly the first time losing him had crossed my mind.

Unable to stop myself, I relaxed against his chest and allowed his arms to wrap around me.

He held me there until I fell asleep. I stirred when he stood but feigned sleep when I realized what he was doing. My father—my cold, often-cruel, complicated father—was carrying me to my room as if I were a small child.

The climb up the stairs was easy for him, and he kissed my forehead as he tucked me beneath the blankets. He paused in the doorway as he left, turning back over his shoulder to whisper, "I love you" in Gaelic.

I was wide awake now—shaking and sobbing beneath the covers. It should've been healing for my father to confess such feelings to me after years of wanting to hear such words. Instead, it terrified me.

It felt so very much like goodbye.

Chapter 23

The next morning, I woke to Alasdair shaking my shoulders. He was trembling with excitement, and I knew before I opened my eyes that Elspeth had finally told him about the baby.

"Morna, lass, I've news to tell ye. Elspeth…she…she's with child again."

I couldn't remember a time when I'd seen him more ecstatic.

Lifting me from the bed with ease, he pulled me into a hug that left my feet dangling a good distance from the floor. He continued to speak into my ear as he spun me around.

"Ye will be an auntie again. She thinks 'tis another boy, though I doona know how she could possibly know. I doona care if the babe comes out half-horse, I shall love it. Always before, when she's lost them, 'twas earlier in the pregnancy. She has much hope that this one shall live."

Finally, he set me down. I steadied myself as I smiled at him. I didn't tell him that I already knew. It was fitting that he believe himself the first to know.

"'Tis the happiest news I've heard in some time. What do ye think wee Eoin will think of it?"

161

Alasdair laughed and moved to the window. Down below, Eoin was readying his pony to go out on a ride with his grandfather.

"I expect he'll be excited enough until the babe arrives. After that, I willna be surprised if years pass before he makes his peace with having less attention."

It would certainly be an adjustment for the sweet, spoiled child, but there was nothing better than having a sibling with whom to share your childhood. Alasdair had told me many times that he wished we were closer in age so that we could've grown up together. By the time I arrived, Alasdair was nearly grown.

"There will always be plenty of people around the castle to give Eoin attention, so perhaps he willna mind the child as much as ye think."

I leaned in to hug my brother once again. Alasdair's smile was contagious. His happiness pushed away the dreadful feelings I'd fallen asleep with.

"I'm happy for ye, brother. And for Elspeth. And even for myself. Being an aunt has been one of the greatest joys of my life. Have ye told Father yet?"

Alasdair shook his head and pulled away to head toward the door.

"No. I mean to join them on their ride and tell them both at once. Eoin watches Father so closely. If he shows that he is glad and happy about the news, mayhap Eoin will feel the same."

Alasdair all but skipped out of my room. I was still smiling long after he'd gone.

By mid-day, everyone in and around the castle had heard the wonderful news, and happy chatter abounded. The sudden distraction allowed me time to roam the halls of the castle undisturbed. I spent most of the day working through my own thoughts.

I loved Jerry. I could no longer deny the truth of it to myself. I could also no longer deny that it didn't matter at all. I could never have him. I would never see him again.

What then was I to do?

I would be married by the end of the year whether I liked it or not. Was Henry the man I wished to marry?

I didn't love him—of that, I was almost certain. While I enjoyed his company well enough, my mind rarely thought of him when apart from him, and I didn't feel the same innate terror at the thought of losing him that I still felt when I thought of Jerry.

I enjoyed his company and conversation. I found him charming and attractive and perplexing in a way that piqued my interest. I was sure I would never be bored in a life with him and that at least was something.

There was also the undeniable fact that my body enjoyed his company to the point of making me feel shameful from the desire he stirred in me. While Henry had always remained semi-polite and gentlemanly, if ever the day came when he asked me to do something entirely indecent, I wasn't altogether sure I would deny him.

I think the possibility of such a request made the allure of him even greater. When in the presence of my brother or father or anyone else really, Henry was the epitome of all things proper.

When alone, he couldn't keep his hands off me. I didn't want him to.

A life with Henry would be filled with surprises, splendid conversation, and if our passion in kissing was any indication, spectacular love making. Most people would only ever dream of such a match.

Even if my heart would never love him in the way I wished it would, by the time the sun began to set over Conall Castle, I'd made my decision.

I would be a fool to send Henry away. I would tell him at dinner that I wished to be his bride.

"**D**o ye mean it, lass? Ye shall make me the happiest man alive."

I decided to tell Henry just as everyone gathered for dinner so that he could make the announcement over our meal. He appeared excited by my decision but not the least bit surprised.

I don't think he'd ever doubted that I would eventually say yes.

"Aye, I'll marry ye. I thought ye could tell everyone tonight."

"I doona wish to wait a moment. Let us tell them now."

Grabbing my hand, Henry led me into the dining hall where Father, Alasdair, Elspeth, and Eoin sat gathered around the table. Mary stood in the corner of the room, waiting for us to sit so she could summon the other servants to bring out the food.

Henry didn't waste a moment.

"Today is the happiest of days. Not only have we learned that a new child is to be welcomed into yer family, but I now know that I shall have the privilege of joining ye, as well. Morna has finally agreed to be my wife."

The reaction around the room was far more mixed than I anticipated. While Eoin began clapping in ignorant delight and Father stood to hug us both, everyone else looked as if I'd just punched them.

I heard Mary drop something in the back of the room. Elspeth glanced down at the table as if to hide her expression, and Alasdair's face gave nothing away. My brother's eyes locked with mine in a steadfast gaze that held a thousand questions.

Father carried on his congratulations with such enthusiasm that dinner was able to progress without Henry taking notice of the subdued responses from everyone else. I couldn't eat a bite. Not with the way Alasdair continued to stare at me throughout the meal. Before everyone was even finished, Alasdair stood.

"Morna, I've something of Mother's I wish to give ye. She'd want ye to have it now that ye are betrothed."

It was the perfect excuse, but I knew there was no gift awaiting me outside the room. Nerves settling deep inside me, I followed my brother outside.

"Ye've a habit of pulling me away from dinner."

Ignoring me, Alasdair turned and sat down on one of the stairwell steps. I joined him.

"Are ye sure about this, lass? Ye doona have to marry him."

I nodded.

"Aye, I do. Father has made it clear that I must marry. Ye know if I send Henry away, Ludo Buchanan will come. If he's

165

anything like ye described him to be, I'm quite certain I'd rather die than marry him. Henry is a proper choice. I've made up my mind."

Alasdair sighed. "I want so much more for ye than a 'proper choice.' I want ye to love as I have loved."

Reaching my hand to soothe him, I patted my brother's back. "We canna all be as lucky as ye and Elspeth. Doona worry for me. I'm settled in my decision."

"Does that mean ye've told him, then? He knows of yer magic and ye trust him with it?"

My hand stilled on his back. I would never tell anyone of my magic ever again. I wanted nothing to do with it.

"No."

"Ye must tell him, Morna. I doona know what happened between ye and Jerry, but I am no fool. His departure injured ye in a way that turned ye away from magic. Ye know ye doona have that choice—magic is not something that ye can either take or leave. It will always be a part of ye.

"When ye doona practice, when ye doona continue to learn, the power builds up inside ye. Ye canna hide it from Henry forever. If ye are willing to trust yer life to him, ye must trust this secret to him, as well."

Alasdair stood, kissed the top of my head, and left me with the only ultimatum I'd ever heard escape his lips.

"'Twould be unfair to both of ye to wed and keep this a secret. I'll give ye three days, lass. If ye doona tell him by then, I'll do it myself."

Chapter 24

E very day following Alasdair's ultimatum, I tried to tell Henry.

On the first day, I took him riding—something I rarely did. I much preferred walking, but I hoped the distance away from the castle might give me the courage to tell him.

Instead, I only ended up with a sore arse and a bad mood.

On the second day, I casually mentioned the use of magic and asked what his opinion was. His response did nothing to ease my nerves.

He said, "*I doona know what to think of those who claim to possess such magic. 'Tis much like ghosts, I believe. Until I see one myself, I canna say anything either way. Though, if I do ever see a witch, it might frighten me enough that I run them through with a sword. The very thought of another changing anything with simple words makes me uneasy.*"

So not only did the thought of magic make him uneasy, but he also considered killing witches a plausible option if seeing one. It didn't bode well.

By day three, I was resolute in my determination to tell him. I couldn't possibly let Alasdair be the one to reveal it to him.

I woke early in the morning, dressed, and after making certain that neither Father nor Alasdair were anywhere in the corridor, knocked on the door to Henry's bedchamber.

He opened it with only his kilt on—his chest entirely bare. Every muscle in my body clenched just looking at him, but I couldn't allow myself to be distracted.

"Lass, I never thought I'd see the day when ye would so brazenly knock on my door. What if someone sees ye? 'Twouldn't look good for either of us."

Undeterred, I kept my gaze on his eyes.

"No one will see me for I have no intention of stepping inside yer room. I wish to show ye something. Will ye dress and meet me downstairs?"

Intrigued, he nodded, bent to steal a quick kiss, then closed the door in my face.

I stood on the hidden door to my basement, staring up at Henry, completely unable to say to him what I knew I must.

"Henry, I…there is something I must tell ye, something ye must know if we are to be married."

His patience thinning, Henry reached for my hands and squeezed them gently.

"Aye, I know, lass. Ye've said that three times now. Why doona ye go ahead and tell me what ye must? There is no reason for ye to be frightened. I can think of nothing that could dissuade me from my desire to make ye my bride."

My palms were sweating, and my heart pounded painfully against my ribs.

"Doona say that until ye know what 'tis that I am."

His brows pinched together.

"What ye are, lass? What ye are is the lass I mean to marry."

Nodding, I searched for the words. Then I suddenly realized with such clarity that it dizzied me what my problem was. I wasn't nervous to tell him. I didn't want to. I didn't feel safe.

Tears sprung up in my eyes as I looked up at him and thought of the last time I'd told someone my secret. It had been so different with Jerry. Rather than fear or apprehension, I felt desire—a desire to tell him my deepest secret with no worry that doing so would put me in danger.

I didn't feel that way with Henry. Alasdair was right. How could I possibly marry a man I couldn't trust with the most sacred parts of myself?

Henry noticed the moment something in my gaze shifted. Before I knew it, his hands were on me. It seemed to be his greatest talent—noticing when my mind would distance itself from him—realizing when doubt slipped into my mind. He used his lips as a distraction, and I always succumbed to it.

With his hands bracing my arms, his lips against mine, he moved me until my back touched the castle's outer wall. His lips were rough and demanding, and I melted against him, surrendering to the thrust of his tongue and moaning as his hands roamed my body. There was more persistence in this kiss than most. As his hand slipped beneath the top of my dress, dipping to touch my breast, I gasped and squirmed beneath him.

With each encounter, our level of intimacy grew.

Groaning, he moved his mouth to my ear.

"If ye wished to kiss me, lass, ye dinna have to create a story of some false confession to do it. I'll always touch ye if ye wish it. Ye simply could've entered my room when ye knocked. Ach, the things I could do to ye there."

I allowed my eyes to flutter closed as I relaxed against the wall, exposing my neck as he licked and bit until I was moaning in delight.

The sudden sound of a horse approaching caused my eyes to fling open as all desire left me. Henry heard it, too, and pulled himself away with incredible speed. As he stepped away, I saw the unmanned horse, and my blood ran cold.

Jerry's horse that was notorious for finding ways out of the stables to go roam on his own, slowly approached.

Without a word, I turned and ran to the stables, leaving Henry panting on top of the secret I would never share with him.

The stables lay a good distance from my spell room. By the time I burst through its doors, I was red-faced and breathless. Bending to rest my hands on my knees, I gasped for air. I expected to find Kip, but it was my brother's voice that called to me from the opposite end.

"Morna, lass, what is the matter? Has something happened?"

Standing, I struggled to speak through gasps of air.

"Jerry's...horse..." I took a deep breath. "Did it...did it find its way back here...on its own? Did ye send someone after it?"

I couldn't make sense of any of it. Wouldn't the horse have stayed with the druid's clan?

Alasdair said nothing. He simply shook his head then bobbed it toward the space behind me.

When his hand touched my shoulder, everything grew dizzy as my mind protested against the truth. At the sound of Jerry's voice, my eyes filled with tears.

"I brought the horse back myself. The druid wasna there, and their territory lay much further away than expected."

Fury unlike any I'd ever experienced filled me. With my back still toward Jerry, I pointed to my brother and shooed him from the stables.

"Alasdair, I need ye to leave here and make certain no one else enters until I step outside these stables. I doona ever ask ye for anything. Allow me this time alone with him."

If my brother had suspected what lay between me and Jerry before, my reaction now surely confirmed it, but I couldn't bring myself to care. Graciously, he understood the seriousness in my tone and backed out of the stables without another word.

The moment we were alone I spun, palm open, as I slapped Jerry hard across the face.

Chapter 25

Jerry

The lass could hit with more force than most men. If I wasn't already completely in love with her, I would've fallen for her right then. It knocked me off balance, and I stumbled until I caught myself on a wooden post of one of the stalls. When I steadied myself, her eyes were as vibrantly green as I remembered them, though there was more fire in their center, and the heat of her anger was palpable.

I would allow her to scream and release her anger however she wanted. Her rage could never match the anger I felt at myself for being such a fool. As my vision cleared, I looked her over more carefully. My eyes stopped at her chest. Her gown was pulled loose, her breasts nearly exposed. I wanted to kill the man that had touched her.

She was screaming at me, and the moment I stood upright, she charged me again, her fists pounding against my chest as I moved to find support from the wall. She was sobbing, and her words came between gasping breaths.

"Ye were gone. How dare ye...how dare ye come back here? Everything ye said...the last words between us...ye made it clear I wouldna see ye again."

I grabbed her wrists and pulled her arms against me, holding her close. She looked hard into my eyes, and all I wanted to do was kiss her. Even angry and sobbing, she was the most beautiful lass in this century or any other. I refrained from doing so. I worried that in her anger, she might bite my tongue off.

My words were foolish, but my own anger rose the more I looked at her exposed chest. It made me angry at myself for encouraging her to move on.

"Do ye wish me to leave again? Ye are nearly as undressed as I found ye in yer bedchamber so many nights ago. 'Tis clear ye dinna miss me at all."

Magic slipped from her as my words filled her with more rage. Fire shot through my hands, scalding me as I released my grip on her. Astonished at how much her powers had grown in just a few weeks, I watched on with amazement as she screamed at me.

Morna

Only twice before had my emotions caused magic to leave me unbidden, but as Jerry accused me of callously moving on, I could no longer control the waves of power coursing through me. There was nothing conscious about the magic that left me. One moment he held me tight against him. The next moment heat soared through my hands, pushing him and pinning him away from me.

He didn't seem frightened and didn't try to move as I continued to release every feeling inside me.

"Doona ye pretend to know how I did or dinna miss ye. Ye've no idea the pain yer leaving caused me. And ye dare to chastise me for doing precisely what ye ordered me to. Eight weeks ye said…eight weeks and I should marry another.

"All I thought of for eight weeks was ye. And even then, I couldna bring myself to believe ye'd truly gone. Even if ye'd found the druid, I thought ye would return here and allow me to send ye back once I learned how.

"I held on to hope for far too long. I even found ye, Jerry. I cast a spell, and I saw ye there…at yer home…in yer own time. 'Twas only then that I truly said goodbye to ye, and it broke my heart to do so."

He started to speak but I interrupted before he could finish.

"What did…"

"No, Jerry. I'm speaking. Ye dinna allow me a word when ye left so I will speak all that I wish to now. Everything is yer fault. I couldna even bring myself to practice magic after ye left. I thought ye were my friend. I thought ye cared. I would never treat someone I cared about as ye treated me."

The more I spoke, the more my anger abated. When I was finally finished, all I felt was a deep empty ache inside.

He allowed the silence to hang between us until I released him from the spell that held him pinned. When he was free, he neared me slowly, hesitantly, as if he was afraid I would spook like an unbroken horse.

"Lass, I dinna return to my own time. I already told ye the druid was not in Allen territory. They'd not seen him in some time. What did ye see that made ye believe I was gone from here?"

The vision had been so clear that I'd never questioned it. But, of course, if Jerry was here now, it couldn't possibly have been true. What then had I seen?

I allowed him to take my hands as I thought back on the vision. I took my time in relaying every detail of it to him. When I finished, Jerry kissed both of my palms as he spoke gently.

"I doona claim to know much of magic, but I know from my time with Grier just how fickle it can be. Ye said that ye placed me at the center of yer mind. I believe that ye did, but mayhap yer question was different than ye believed it to be. Mayhap what ye saw was not where I was at that time, but where I will one day be. Mayhap it was proof that ye will find a way to see me home."

Jerry's suggestion did little to mend the ache inside me. If he was correct, then it simply meant I would be forced to lose him all over again. That even after returning here, he still wished to return to his time and leave me. It angered me and tugged at my already shredded heart. The past few days had been disastrously difficult. I no longer wanted to be near him.

If he was here, I would help him, but getting close to him would only make it more difficult once I found a way to get him home.

"Let go of me, Jerry. 'Tis unkind of ye to mislead me as ye do."

He didn't release his grip, and I did little to try and move away.

"Mislead ye, lass? How do ye think I've done that?"

I was so tired of crying. I didn't want him to see how much I cared, but my voice was choked as I answered him.

"Each time ye touch me, I feel as if ye want me. Ye are jealous of men who desire me, but ye doona want me for yerself. I am worth more than that, Jerry. Ye take advantage of my own feelings for ye, but ye still wish to return to yer own time. Ye still wish to leave me."

"No." He reached up to brush the tears from my cheeks. "Ye are wrong. For some time now, I've cared nothing about returning to my own time. I know what I said when I left. I was a damned fool for saying what I did, but I dinna go after the druid for me. I went after him because I believe just as strongly as yer brother does that ye need help growing yer powers. I went there for ye, lass, but I'll not be going anywhere without ye again."

I wanted so desperately to believe him, but his own words had already contradicted him.

"Jerry, ye just said that I must have seen yer future in the spell. Ye know then that ye still leave here. If ye truly care for me as much as ye say ye do, 'twould not be the future I would have seen."

He smiled and moved one hand through my hair so that he held the back of my neck.

"Ye also said there was a woman. I've no wife, lass. Mayhap the shadow ye saw was ye."

I would never leave my own time. I loved my brother and nephew and friends too much.

"No. I canna ever leave here, Jerry. I doona want to."

He nodded and pulled my head closer to his own.

"In my experience, 'tis best to never swear off anything. But lass, if ye stay here, so shall I. I can promise ye that. I mean to kiss ye now. 'Tis all I've dreamt of since I left. Please doona deny me."

Just as Jerry's lips neared mine, my father's voice bellowed from the end of the stables.

"Jerry, are ye in there, lad? Alasdair told me ye'd returned. We've all missed ye."

I exhaled, realizing that the shadows had prevented him from seeing us. Stepping into the light, I called to him.

"Aye, Father, he's here. I came to welcome him back myself."

Nearing Jerry, my father met him with a hug.

"Did she tell ye all of the good news, lad? So much has happened while ye were away. Mary and Kip were married. Elspeth and Eoin are expecting another child, and Morna has found herself betrothed."

Jerry looked as if he'd been stabbed as he stepped out of my father's embrace. His eyes were cold as he looked at me.

"No, she told me nothing."

Father didn't pick up on the sudden tension between us. Slapping Jerry's back, he took my arm and began to lead me from the stables.

"Ach, well we are all glad ye've returned. I need ye and Kip to ready my and Henry's horses. We leave at sunset on a hunting trip to celebrate his betrothal to Morna."

Chapter 26

Everyone gathered to see Father and Henry off on their hunting trip. They planned to be away three days, and I found myself eager to see them gone. I needed distance from Henry to decide the best way to end things. I couldn't marry him. Even if Jerry hadn't returned, the moment with him above my spell room had sealed it. I couldn't marry someone who caused me to seize up so completely when trying to reveal one of the most important parts of myself.

Jerry cast angry glances in my direction when Henry neared me as we all joined near the stables to say our goodbyes. I ignored them each and every time. I wouldn't allow myself to feel guilty for anything that had transpired between Henry and me, and I couldn't very well behave as if we were anything other than betrothed in front of everyone.

"I'll miss ye, lass. When I return, we shall make plans to ride to my territory and for the wedding."

I wouldn't show him false enthusiasm, but I wouldn't be unkind to him. He'd done nothing to deserve it. "Doona let my father intimidate ye. He likes to behave as if he is a better hunter than he is."

He moved in to kiss me. Although I stiffened, I allowed the brief touch of his lips.

As he went to mount his horse, Jerry stomped away. I suspected it was so he wouldn't be tempted to shove Henry off the moment he got on.

Father came up to me next. The same dreadful feeling I'd had in front of him a few nights before came flooding back. I opened my arms to him and squeezed him as tightly as I could.

An urgency I couldn't explain filled me, and I hurried to return the words he'd shared with me in my bedchamber.

"I love ye, Father. Be safe. Doona venture into parts of the woods ye doona know."

He kissed the top of my head before pulling away.

"I love ye, too, lass. I'll stay to the woods I know if ye agree to stay on castle grounds while I'm away. Doona go into the village."

For the first time in my life, Father's protectiveness felt more like a gift and less like a burden. I nodded in agreement as he walked away.

We all stood huddled in a group as we waved them off. When we could no longer see them, Jerry approached. I was in no mood to speak with him.

"Stay away from me. Do ye think I wished to agree to marry him? Ye've no one to blame but yerself. Now, I must spend the day pondering how to break the engagement without causing a clash between our two clans."

"Do ye need some help, lass? I'm certain we can find a solution together. I canna bear for that man to put his lips on ye again."

I wanted to be alone—entirely alone—for the next three days.

"No. If ye come near me, I'll hit ye again."

At least Jerry had the wits to withhold his laughter until he was too far away for me to strike him.

Time alone did little to encourage any plan that seemed worthy. I ended up spending most of my time lounging in bed, reading, and calling servants to have warm bath water brought to my chambers. If I couldn't think of a good solution, I could at least allow myself to be a little indulgent while Father was away.

On the second night of their trip, I lay soaking in a quickly-cooling tub of water when the handle to my bedchamber door turned.

"Eoin, if 'tis ye lad, I need ye to stay outside. Go and demand that yer da play with ye. I'll find ye in a while."

The door to my bedchamber opened despite my protest, and Jerry stepped casually inside.

I sloshed more than a little water out onto the floor in an effort to cover myself.

"Get out of here this instant or I'll scream. Ye canna just enter a lassie's bedchamber any time ye wish it."

He leaned against the door, crossed his arms, and stared back at me as if he were bored.

"Ye willna scream, for ye know I willna glance in the water nor touch ye unless ye wish it. Ye've avoided me for well over a day now. I decided 'twas worth risking another beating to see ye."

A beating was a rather dramatic way to describe it—his face showed no signs of my palm.

"I told ye I wished to be alone."

"Aye, I know, and why is that precisely? I have my suspicions."

Sometimes Jerry was infuriatingly sure of his ability to read me.

"Ye have suspicions?"

"Aye, I do. I think ye want me so badly that ye are frightened to be near me. I think ye know that if we were to spend time together while yer father and Henry are away, I would end up in yer bed, and ye doona wish to carry a guilty conscience for bedding one man whilst engaged to another."

I was suddenly far too aware of the nakedness of my body and Jerry's close proximity to it. While he may not have been able to see down into the water now, only a few steps prevented him being able to see every inch of me.

"I can assure ye that no such thought has entered my mind. Please leave me so that I might dress."

"I'll leave ye, but the moment ye are dressed, I intend to step back inside this room."

Relief washed over me, and I loosened the grip on my breasts just a bit.

"Whatever for?"

"To kiss ye, lass. To kiss ye until every memory of Henry's lips on ye are washed clean from yer mind. Ye doona mind his touch. I could see it in the way ye leaned into his kiss yesterday. 'Twas not like Seumas' kiss where ye tolerated it simply to torture me. Part of ye enjoys Henry's touch. I canna sleep until I know I've changed that."

I couldn't tell if I began to tremble in anticipation or from the cooling water, but when Jerry stepped out into the hallway, I was trembling all over.

I dried myself quickly and glanced around the room with terror over what I should dress in. A full gown was foolish this late in the evening—to place on my nightgown was inviting trouble.

With Henry, I wouldn't have dreamed of it. With Jerry, it was all I wanted.

For with him, even trouble seemed relatively safe. He would protect and cherish me, and it was all I'd wanted for months.

Taking a breath for courage, I slipped on my sleeping gown and opened the door to let him inside.

Chapter 27

"**D**o ye wish me to leave, lass? I doona..." Jerry reluctantly pulled his hand away from my leg, allowing my nightgown to fall back toward the ground. He lay his forehead gently against my own, his breathing ragged, his voice pained. "If ye doona want this, send me away from here. I want too much from ye—things ye may not be ready to give."

He was perilously close to doing so much more than just kissing any memory of Henry from my mind. In truth, he'd already succeeded. I would never be able to kiss or look at Henry the same way again, but Jerry was holding on to his resolve to be respectful of me with so much fervor it was physically painful for him.

My mind had been made up the moment I opened the door. There was no turning back—not this night—quite possibly, not ever.

I reached up and placed my palms on his face, lifting his head up so I could look at him. Leaning forward, I whispered in his ear.

"What is it ye want, Jerry? Tell me. I want to know."

He pulled back, his face suddenly serious.

"Did ye sleep with him, lass? Ye doona seem..." He faltered, searching for the right words. "Well, ye doona seem like a nervous virgin."

I smiled and kissed him gently on the cheek before stepping away to stand across from him.

"Jerry, ye have met Mary, havena ye? I learned much about what happens in the beds of lovers at a far younger age than was proper. I know what this night can be between us. I wouldna have let ye inside this room if I dinna want it. Ye were right that night ye came into my bedchamber after I kissed Seumas. I wasted my first kiss. I doona wish to waste this."

His expression softened as he exhaled a deep, shaky breath.

"Ach, thank God, lass. I dinna know for certain. I hoped," he paused and raked his hand through his hair. "God, I hoped, but with the way the lad looks at ye, I worried ye'd bedded him."

He stepped toward me, reached for my hands, and pulled me hard against him, whispering into my ear as I allowed my front to press against his chest.

"Ye do know I love ye, doona ye, lass?"

I trembled as his lips touched my neck. When his hand cupped my breast, I moaned.

"I hoped. I dinna know."

His hand slid from my chest, up my neck, and to my face where he held me gently, his thumb sweeping soft strokes over my cheek.

"I have loved ye since I opened my eyes in that riverbed to see ye staring at me with those wide, green eyes. For so long, I wondered why this happened to me—why I was chosen to fall through time and leave everything in my old life. The moment I saw ye, I knew. We were meant for one another."

186

Why had I kept the truth from him? His absence was no excuse. I'd known long before that, but for so long I tried to deny it myself. Did the spell Grier and I cast so many years ago make our love for one another any less real? I worried that maybe it did. Or at the very least, that Jerry would believe it did.

Could I confess my love for him while holding this secret? Not if I wanted to sleep easily at night.

The feel of his lips across my collarbone begged me to surrender to the sensation, to relinquish my need to tell him what I knew.

"Jerry, there is something I must tell ye."

He continued to caress and kiss and hold me tight against him. His words dragged across my skin as he spoke between kisses.

"Tell me later, lass. I canna promise I will remember a word ye say to me now. I canna think with ye in my arms."

I pulled away to put some distance between us. He needed to hear me. Once he knew, it might change his feelings.

"If I doona tell ye now, I doona trust myself to ever tell ye."

"What is it, lass? Nothing can be as bad as ye are making it seem."

"Aye, 'tis." I was so much more nervous to tell him this than I was at the thought of sleeping with him. "I believe it might be my fault, Jerry. I may have spelled ye here. It might have been me that pulled ye from yer home." I couldn't keep my voice from breaking.

"Morna." Jerry moved to stand in front of me, gathered my hands in his own, and ushered me over to the bed where we sat at its edge. His eyes were kind and calm. "I doona mean to offend ye, lass, but seeing as ye havena been able to find a way

187

to see me home yet, I doona believe ye were the one who pulled me from it."

Looking down to avoid his eyes, I spoke.

"'Twasn't my spell, though I was a willing participant. 'Twas Grier's."

I heard his breath catch and didn't dare look up to see his face.

"'Tis not possible. Grier dinna possess such knowledge. I spent a year with her while she tried to find a way to send me home. She wouldna have done that if she'd known how."

Still gazing downward, I shook my head. "I'm not so certain, Jerry. I know that 'twas she who sent ye back in time."

"How do ye know that, lass?"

I told him everything about my last day with Grier, taking care to describe the man I saw in the mirror so he would know it was him. When I finished, his hand cupped my chin and gently lifted my head so I would look at him.

"Why did ye tell me this?"

Of course I felt responsible. If only I had told Grier *no* that day, Jerry wouldn't have been pulled so suddenly from his home. His entire life wouldn't have been upended without his consent.

"How could I not tell ye? Jerry, I love ye. I've loved ye for some time now, but what if the only reason we care for one another is Grier's spell? What if 'tis magic and not truth that binds us together?"

"Magic done through love is truth, lass. I canna begin to understand why Grier lied to me for so long—why she dinna bring me straight here if she knew this was where I was meant to be. But I do know this: Grier cast that spell on the day she left

188

because she loved ye and she wanted ye to be loved. I doona believe she found me and spelled me to love ye. I believe she looked into yer heart and saw what was destined to be."

He paused and moved in to kiss me. His lips were soft, slow, and gentle. Each moment with him holding me allowed one more ounce of anxiety to melt away. Trailing his lips toward my ear, he whispered, "I doona care how I got here, lass. I love ye. 'Tis all that truly matters. Allow me to show ye what 'tis to be bedded by a man who loves ye. Close yer eyes."

His lips touched my lids as I closed them. Slowly his hands grazed the sides of my neck, his mouth trailing quickly behind them as he continued to drag his hands down my body. The fabric of my gown was thin. As he cupped my breast, his thumb flicking the rounded tip of my nipple, I gasped and arched backward.

Eyes flickering open, I reached for his head to try and pull his mouth to mine.

He pulled away.

"I doona even have my hands on yer bare skin yet, lass. I mean to take my time with ye. If ye continue to breathe like that, I willna be able to. Close yer eyes and let all thought leave ye. Just feel my touch. Respond to it in kind."

Smiling, I closed my eyes again and lay back on the bed, my knees and feet dangling off its side. I gasped once more as his fingers brushed the uncovered skin of my leg. He swept his hand up my leg with one quick touch, and my thighs opened instinctively, welcoming the sudden sensation of his fingers trailing across my center.

"I need to see ye."

Lifting my hips, he scooted the bottom of my gown up until he could drag it underneath me. I should've felt exposed knowing he was about to see me naked. All I felt was anticipation.

"Look at me, lass."

I felt his weight on top of me, and I opened my eyes to see him straddled over me, the bottom of my gown in both hands as he worked it up and behind my back. I lifted my head to allow him to pull it off me completely.

I smiled as I followed his gaze to my breasts. I'd never seen such blatant admiration on someone's face before. It sent a flash of heat rushing through my body. Even without past experience to guide me, I felt empty without him. I wanted him inside me, claiming me. I wanted to be responsible for his pleasure.

He looked down at my breasts for a long moment. Before I could say anything, he lifted himself and went to stand at the edge of the bed.

"Sorry lass, I canna bear to have clothes on a moment more. I need to feel my skin against yer own."

Lifting myself up to my elbows, I watched him undress. He removed his kilt with little effort. As the thick fabric fell to the floor, he removed his linen shirt. I felt my cheeks warm. It was the first time in my life I'd seen a naked man.

The definition in his muscular body surprised me. I'd always known he was strong, but feeling his strength and seeing it were two very different things.

"Ye are the most beautiful man I've ever seen."

His nose scrunched up as he laughed.

"Doona call me beautiful, lass."

I smiled and motioned for him to join me on the bed. The space between us felt too vast.

"But ye are. 'Tis the only word that comes to mind. I am in awe of ye. I want ye inside me."

The noise that escaped his throat was one of pure guttural need. His eyes darkened, and he swallowed as he approached the bed.

"Lass, I already told ye, I mean to take my time with ye. When ye say things like that, ye make it verra difficult for me to hold on to my determination."

I didn't want to be bedded by someone restraining his every thought and movement. I wanted our lovemaking to be a mutually-shared moment where each of us could release everything and simply be with the other.

As he neared the bed, I sat up so I could wrap my arms around his neck. Before he could protest or push me away, I pressed my breasts against his chest and slowly kissed his neck. Feeling him melt against me, I unwound one hand and dragged it down the front of his body to touch his hardened manhood.

He gasped and went rigid.

"Morna, lass, please. I beg ye, remove yer hand. Lie back and let me take my time with ye."

I continued to hold on and gently ran my hand up and down him as he buckled slightly in front of me.

"No, Jerry. I know ye mean to be kind to me, to be gentle, but 'tis not what I want. I doona wish for ye to think about how ye must be or what ye should do. I just want ye to be here with me. Do what ye will. I'll do the same. Let us freely enjoy one another."

My words freed him, and I happily opened myself up to him as he crushed himself against me.

Every sensation was new, every touch a discovery. The pain I felt at his entry was nothing compared to the wave of pleasure that washed over me shortly after.

Our first time was rough, fast, and clumsy.

Our second time was slow and sweet.

By the early hours of the morning, I'd lost count of the number of times we sought to discover joys in the other. Each one was perfect in its uniqueness.

My world was now so very different.

I was a woman entirely in love.

Chapter 28

We slept on and off through the night, waking every few hours. We would then visit before making love again. As the sun began to peek through the night sky, we both knew it was time to decide what we must do next. Our night of pretending as if we were the only two people in the world was ending.

"I wish to marry ye, lass. As soon as we can see to it, if ye'll have me. I want ye as my wife."

Laying with my head on his chest, I looked up and smiled at him.

"O'course I'll have ye. Do ye think I would have done everything we just did, if I dinna plan to marry ye?"

He laughed against my hair.

"Aye, I do. Ye wanted me that badly. What should we do? I fear when ye tell Henry he willna handle it well."

"He willna be pleased, but I've no reason to believe that he willna be gracious."

Shifting me off him, Jerry sat up in the bed.

"Ye still canna see it, can ye? I doona believe Henry is a good man. I doona say that because the thought of his hands on ye causes my blood to boil. I know ye say he's been good to ye, but all men can be good for a time if it gets them what they want. What he wants is ye, lass. Now that ye've agreed to marry him, he believes ye are his."

"Ye believe his behavior will change now that we are betrothed?"

Jerry nodded, his fingers tracing lazy circles down my arm.

"Once he has ye away from yer brother and father, once ye are at his home around his servants, aye. He yelled at Kip yesterday as we readied their horses. 'Twas the temper of a man well-practiced in cruelty."

I thought of Elspeth and the scene we'd witnessed from her bedchamber window.

"Henry can do nothing to me as long as I'm here. 'Tis Father who concerns me. He willna care for me breaking my word."

"Would he..." Jerry's voice lowered as he asked, "Would he ever permit ye to marry me?"

"No."

I hated my answer, but I knew it was true. Father saw it as his duty to see me cared for in a manner he felt acceptable. Jerry had no rank in class and no home of his own.

"Then what are we to do? I know ye willna leave here. I would never ask ye to run away with me."

He was right. I would never leave my home forever, but for a time, perhaps it would be bearable. I could think of no other way we could be together.

"We could enlist Alasdair's help. 'Twill place him in a terrible position, but I know he will help us. He cares for ye. As long as I am happy and loved, he doesna care who I marry."

I pushed myself up and twisted to face Jerry. Every inch of my body ached deliciously.

"What assistance can he provide?"

I thought for a moment, trying to work through every possible outcome in my mind. No solution was ideal, but unless I wished to leave for McCabe Castle in a matter of days, we would have to do something.

"He can help us marry in secret and see that Henry returns to his home without a dispute breaking out between our two clans. Henry is his friend. I know he can talk to him. With time, Father will have to accept what we've done. If we are married, he willna have a choice."

He did have a choice. He could always disown me and order me to never return home. But as long as Alasdair lived, I knew my brother would never allow it.

Jerry didn't seem pleased with the suggestion. His face was solemn—his eyes sad.

"I doona wish to take ye from yer family, lass. Perhaps, we shouldna marry. Perhaps, ye should send Henry away and every suitor after. 'Twill pain me to see ye in the presence of any other man, but I'd rather have ye in secret than tear apart yer family."

It was an outrageous suggestion.

"I canna bear to have suitor after suitor welcomed into this castle when I know my heart belongs to ye. We must think of another way."

We discussed various possibilities until the night was long gone and sunlight filled the room. Eventually though, with the appearance of no plausible solution, we fell asleep wrapped in each other's arms.

"**M**orna, wake up. Ye must wake up. 'Tis urgent."

I stirred to the touch of someone's hands on my shoulders and opened my eyes to find Elspeth standing next to my bed. I scrambled to cover myself and immediately flew into an attempt to explain Jerry's presence in my bed. She interrupted me before I could even start.

"It doesna matter, lass. Not now. It doesna matter. Something terrible has happened."

Jerry stirred beside me, his face turning oddly white as he looked at Elspeth.

It was only then that I could see the concern on her face.

"What is it? What's happened?"

"'Tis yer father, Morna. He's dead."

Chapter 29

J erry couldn't believe it. His reaction, once Elspeth left us, was to deny its truth. He dressed and paced around the room murmuring words meant to comfort me.

"They are not back yet. She heard this through the word of others. Perhaps he is merely injured. He'll be fine once he is home."

I knew Father was gone. I could feel it—the lack of his energy in the world. While I'd tried to deny and ignore the feeling, I knew this was coming.

I felt nothing, only a cool numbness that slowed the movement in my mind. I needed to see Alasdair. I needed to speak to him, to see if he was okay, to see what we would do now. Both our lives had always revolved around our father. What would our lives look like now? There would be much to take care of.

It surprised me how methodically my thinking became—so detached, so distant, as if I were an outsider sent here to help my family through this. I dressed slowly. I took my time pinning my hair and rinsing my face. When I was ready, I turned to Jerry and asked him to leave.

"I must find Alasdair. Go see to Mary and Kip. She will be devastated, and she will need extra help in whatever preparations must be made."

He stared at me a long moment. I knew he was trying to gauge whether he should gather me in his arms to comfort me or do as I asked.

Crossing the room to him, I squeezed his hand like I would that of a child.

"I'm fine. We will speak of all of this later."

I went in search of my brother.

My cold feeling of detachment vanished the moment I found Alasdair sitting by the fire in the sitting room. It was as if I simply couldn't allow the reality to set in until I was with him. It was a grief we were meant to share together.

As he stood, I ran to him, allowing him to gather me in his arms as we wept together.

I knew both of us had such complicated emotions regarding our father. But in the end, every negative thing I ever felt about him didn't seem to matter. All I felt was love for him and a deep sense of loss that seemed as if it would never end.

"He died in his sleep, just like Grandmother."

"He dinna seem ill. Though, I think mayhap he knew his death was near."

His arms still wrapped protectively around me, Alasdair rubbed my back gently. "How do ye mean, lass?"

I told him of my last conversations with Father, of the tenderness he'd shown me, of the dread I felt when he left. When Alasdair spoke, his voice was filled with emotion.

"I canna tell ye how much peace it brings me to know that. I've always worried he would leave this earth filled with regret for how he treated ye. 'Tis a blessing that in the end he shared with ye how he really felt."

I cried into my brother's chest as we clung to each other. "If it would've been less painful, I think mayhap I would've preferred for him to stay unkind. Losing him feels as if it may rip me apart."

"We shall both heal from this, lass. I will hold ye together, and yer faith in me will keep me strong, just as we have always done for one another."

"How is Eoin?"

Alasdair sighed. I could feel the burden he was already beginning to bear. He would see everyone through this, be the pillar of strength for everyone in and around the castle. He would be the best laird Conall territory had ever seen.

"I doona know how much the wee lad understands. He will miss him dearly. He was the only person whom Father softened around. He spoiled Eoin immensely."

Grief is so much more than the unbearable sense of loss. It throws you off course, makes everything seem so unsure.

"What do we do now, Alasdair?"

"First," he paused and pulled away to look down at me, "we must discuss Henry."

I felt guilty that he'd not crossed my mind before now.

"O'course. He must be dreadfully upset to have found him."

"'Twas a terrible shock for him, though 'tis not what I meant."

By the way Alasdair stared at me, I could see that he knew.

"I canna marry him."

With understanding in his gaze, he nodded. "I know, lass. Elspeth told me how she found ye this morning. Ye love him, aye? I could see it in yer eyes when ye learned he'd returned."

"Are ye angry?"

He looked confused. "Why would I be angry with ye? Jerry is a good man. If ye love him, 'tis all that matters to me."

I couldn't deny the relief I felt. Every problem Jerry and I struggled with last night was now gone. All we needed to worry about was finding a way to break my engagement to Henry. Would I take every problem back to have Father alive and well again? Of course, but that could never be.

"I do love him. Might we stay here at the castle once we are wed?"

"'Twould break my heart if ye left. Though I think it best if ye keep yer distance from Jerry until after Father's burial. Henry will insist on remaining here until then. We will speak to Henry together after that."

It wasn't Alasdair's duty to end things between Henry and me.

"I shall speak to him alone, but I will wait until afterwards." I couldn't bring myself to say burial.

Alasdair smiled in spite of his tears. "Morna, I have only one request if ye intend to live here."

There was nothing I wouldn't do for him. "Anything."

"In time, ye must return to yer magic. I shall make Conall territory a place that is safe for ye to practice openly. Ye canna continue to deny who ye are."

It seemed improper to feel such relief. I was free to marry Jerry, free to live in the home I knew and loved, free to learn and practice magic without fear of punishment. Why did the moment everything seemed to be falling into place have to be shared with such deep grief?

Chapter 30

We waited three days to bury Father. I spent most of that time alone, crying and working through feelings I didn't know I had for him. By the time it came for everyone to gather, I no longer had tears to shed.

Henry checked on me every day, but the state of my grief made him so uncomfortable that it never took much for me to get him to leave. Jerry kept his distance entirely, but I knew it wasn't his choice to do so. Alasdair had spoken to him and asked him to stay away until everything was settled with Henry.

When I saw him standing with Mary and Kip at Father's burial site, he looked terrible, as if he hadn't slept in days. It was the first thing I said to him.

"Are ye ill, Jerry?"

He wanted to reach for me, and I wanted nothing more than to fall into his arms, but Henry stood only steps away.

Whether he was too tired or too emotional to censor his words, I didn't know, but Mary and Kip's presence did nothing to prevent him from answering honestly.

"I canna sleep knowing I'm not there to comfort ye. Ye shouldna be alone in yer grief. I want to help ye, to hold ye, to let ye know that yer pain willna always be so great."

Mary's mouth fell visibly open, and she leaned over to whisper in my ear.

"I doona care if Henry sees ye. If ye doona hug that lad right now, I'll do it meself."

Alasdair, Elspeth, and Eoin still hadn't come down from the castle so I stood mingling with all the villagers, accepting their condolences and being smothered by hugs until Mary pulled me away from the crowd.

"Ye look as weary as I've ever seen ye. Doona exhaust yerself now. Things will only get harder as the day goes on. When ye see him, ye will likely be unable to hold back yer tears."

I knew she was right. I'd yet to see Father's body. While most had already visited him, I hadn't been able to bring myself to go to him. I wasn't sure I could bear seeing him so cold and lifeless.

"Speak to me of something else, Mary. I am weary of grief consuming my every thought."

She smiled, laced her arms with mine, and led me to the back of Mae's inn. It allowed us a view of the castle so we would know when Alasdair and Elspeth were coming. We could join the others then.

"I know precisely what I wish to speak to ye about. I can see by the way the two of ye looked at each other that ye've bedded him. Tell me everything."

For the first time in days, I genuinely smiled.

"Ye have no shame, Mary. Ye do know ye are the only lass I've ever known to speak of such matters so plainly, aye?"

She laughed and nodded. "'Tis something I pride myself on. Now, doona be coy. Ye can say nothing that will shock me."

There was far too much to tell, but there was one instance during my evening with Jerry that I'd been curious to speak to her about for days.

"I do have something I'd like to ask ye in regards…in regards to something he did to me."

Mary's face lit up with glee. "What did he do to ye? Did he tie yer hands to the bed? Did he nip yer arse?"

I doubled over in laughter, and for a fleeting moment, I was able to forget about Father's death. Then as I remembered, guilt filled me. Mary could see it on my face and grabbed my shoulders.

"I know what grief does to ye, lass. The moment ye start to feel anything other than pain, ye worry that 'tis wrong for ye to do so. Doona ever believe guilt when it tugs at ye. Joy is always acceptable. Our misery does the dead no service. They would prefer that we cling to happiness wherever we can find it. Now…" She paused, stepped away, and smiled wide. "I can see that he dinna bite ye, which 'tis a shame if ye ask me. What did he do then?"

"Is it usual for a man to use his tongue to…" I couldn't bring myself to finish my question.

"To give ye pleasure, ye mean? I wouldna say 'tis usual, but it sure is lovely, aye? Count yerself blessed that ye have a man who cares so much about yer pleasure."

I was lucky—in every way.

"Aye, I know I am. I dread what I must do to Henry. He doesna deserve it."

Mary's nose twisted in the same way Elspeth's almost always did in Henry's company.

"I doona know if I'd say that, lass. Ye seem to be of the belief that Henry treats everyone as he does ye. I can assure ye that 'tis not true."

"Do ye think he's as unkind as Father could be?"

It was so strange for me to hear such different stories of Henry. None of them aligned with the man I'd spent so much time with.

"'Tis true that yer father could be unkind, but there was only one version of him. He would treat royalty no differently than he would treat a beggar. Authenticity is important, lass. I doona trust those that put on airs for some and show their worst to others. 'Tis my experience that such people mean to hide something, and 'tis never something good."

Perhaps she was right about Henry—perhaps they all were. It hardly mattered now. By tomorrow he would be headed back to McCabe Castle, and I would never see him again.

The crowd of villagers began to stir. As I glanced up toward the castle, I could see Alasdair, Elspeth, and Eoin riding toward the village.

Mary reached out to squeeze my hand.

"'Tis time, lass. Let us bid him farewell."

It was a somber burial filled with tears. It was easier than I expected to see Father's body. It looked so cold, so unlike him, that I was able to detach myself from all that was happening around me in a way I hadn't expected. It was so much like the first moments right after I learned of his death.

I knew I would quietly fall apart later.

It was only at the end of the service as they lowered Father into the ground that I noticed her. Standing at the edge of the wood, cloak over her head, she remained far from the crowd. With everyone else so caught up in what was happening in front of them, I knew I was the only one that had seen her.

Grier had returned.

Chapter 31

All I could think when I spotted Grier standing in the woods as if she'd never left all those years ago was that I couldn't let Jerry see her. Not yet—not until I'd spoken with her. I felt deeply protective of him. While I'd grieved her absence from my life once, I knew instinctively that she was not the same person I once knew.

After the burial, Grier was no longer visible. I knew she awaited me in the woods. I could feel it.

Jerry stood at the opposite side of the crowd of villagers. I made my way over to him as quickly as I could. I needed to know where he'd be so I could make certain he wouldn't run into Grier. Fortunately, I didn't have to search for an excuse to keep him busy—he already had plans.

"A lad in the village has asked Kip and me for help with a horse. I am so weary I can scarcely stand, though I think 'tis best if I stay away until Henry is gone. Do ye mean to tell him today?"

It wouldn't be as soon as I'd hoped. I would have to speak to Grier first, but I had every intention of ending things with Henry before nightfall.

"Aye."

Jerry nodded, and the line between his brows relaxed.

"Good. I'll return to my cottage later, but for now, I shall spend the day in the village and allow ye and yer brother to see Henry gone from here. He may ask ye what has caused ye to end yer engagement. If he sees me, 'twould only cause unnecessary trouble."

I nodded and turned to leave him, but his hand reached out to stop me.

"Wait, lass. I wish to give ye something. As I told ye earlier, I've not slept much these past nights. I wished to be there for ye and I couldna be, so I wrote some thoughts down for ye. I know it willna be easy for ye to hurt Henry. Ye've a kind heart, and harsh words doona come easily to ye. I hope that reading what I feel for ye will give ye strength."

I smiled at the folded parchment he extended toward me. Squeezing his hand, I slipped it into the bosom of my dress.

"I'll read it as soon as I get back to the castle. I'll see ye when everything is done."

His letter—no matter how eager I was to read it—would have to wait.

An overdue visit with a ghost from my past stood waiting just footsteps away.

She spotted me before I saw her, and her voice was as distinctive and recognizable as ever.

"Ye grew into just the woman I knew ye would—just as beautiful, just as strong, just as naïve, though the last is no fault of yer own."

She stepped from the woods with the grace of the creatures who lived within them. She could blend in anywhere. Her confidence made any place look like her home.

In the eight years since I'd seen her, she'd not aged a day.

When she opened her arms to me, I cautiously approached and allowed her to embrace me.

Her arms wrapped around me, and one hand stroked the back of my hair as she spoke. "I'm sorry about yer father, lass."

"Ye are not. Ye hated him."

She laughed and released me as she stepped away, her long hair blowing around her face wildly.

"Ye are right. I needn't lie to ye. His death is the best thing that shall ever happen to ye. 'Twas inexcusable for him to keep ye from yer magic as he did. I'm glad ye found the journals I left for ye."

As expected, she'd been watching all from afar.

"'Twas ye that led wee Eoin to the books then, aye?"

She nodded.

"O'course. Though I made sure to hide myself from him. I gently guided him with magic."

The thought of Grier's spells directing Eoin in any form filled me with unease. There was a time I would've trusted her with my life. Now, I felt suspicious of everything she said.

"What are ye doing here, Grier? Why, after all this time, have ye returned?"

"Come now, Morna. Ye must know."

I truly didn't. So little of it made sense.

I shook my head and awaited further explanation. She looked at me expectantly but quickly grew frustrated and threw up her hands in exasperation.

"'Tis all for ye, lass. Doona ye remember the spell we cast our last day together? Jerry is the man I saw in yer future."

She said it so casually as if it explained everything.

"Aye, I've known that for some time. Why then did ye keep him away from me for a year, all the while lying to him about yer ability to help him? Why did ye allow him to believe ye were dead? How did ye survive the fire, and where did ye go during that time?"

An unidentifiable expression passed over Grier's face. Distant, shaken, lonely, and most especially, embarrassed. She looked lost and unsure and very unlike herself.

By bringing up all the questions surrounding her strange behavior, I'd triggered memories she'd rather leave forgotten.

She could see by the directness of my gaze that she had little choice, and the sigh she released said so much more about her true age than her appearance ever would.

"Ye've never known what 'tis like to be truly alone, Morna. I hope ye never do. Loneliness is a slow sickness. At first painless, it eats away at ye little by little. When it starts, ye doona even realize it will change ye, but over time—over days, months, and years of having no one to love—ye change, and the person ye once were no longer exists. Ye become the pain ye hold inside ye.

"I wasna lonely the day I cast Jerry for ye, but I was an empty shell by the day he arrived in our time. I lived a full life here at Conall Castle with ye, yer grandmother, and Alasdair. Your father took everything from me the day he sent me away. For years I had nothing and no one. I dinna realize at first, lass, I truly dinna. I'd not thought of our spell in so long that when I first met Jerry, I dinna know who he was.

"When I realized, I told myself every day that I would tell him the truth, that I would bring him to ye and allow him to either live the life he was meant to with ye or send him home as he wished. But I enjoyed his company too much, and over time, the lie became too big.

"'Twas only when that bastard Creedrich set flame to our home that I saw my opportunity to free myself of Jerry. If he thought me dead, fate would see that he found ye, and it did."

She looked as sad and weary as I felt, as if all the tears she possessed had already been shed. My heart ached for her, but her story still left one blaringly large question unanswered.

"I canna tell ye how sorry I am for what my father did to ye. I missed ye for years after ye left. More than once, I thought about running away and searching for ye. But there is still one question I must ask. Forgive me if it sounds callous. If ye meant to free Jerry from ye, why are ye here now?"

"To seek forgiveness for the pain I caused him and for the time I took from the both of ye. I just need to speak to him one last time, and then I'll leave the two of ye be."

A voice deep inside me suspected the lie for what it was, but it was not my right to deny Jerry the chance to speak with her. I would have to let her see him regardless of the dread that settled in the center of my chest.

"He's in the village. He stays in the cottage that was once yer own. I will go and get him. Wait for him there."

Perhaps it was the wind, but I thought I heard her laughing as I walked away.

Chapter 32

Jerry

Grier's arrival at Conall Castle didn't surprise me. I knew the day I learned she still lived that I would see her again, and I spent the days and months leading up to her return reflecting on my time spent with her. I said nothing to Morna, not because I wished to keep the events of that time from her, but because I saw no need to burden her with emotions that were not hers to work through. She was so much like her brother—they both felt the need to carry the pain of others.

Falling in love with Morna taught me much. Sure, I'd fancied a few lassies back in my own time, bedded more than my fair share, but I'd never loved another outside of the love one has for family or the platonic love one has for friends.

The moment I realized the depth of my feelings for Morna was the moment I could see something I should've seen from the start—Grier was in love with me. While my affection for her had been true, she'd only ever been my friend, but that had never been her feelings for me.

215

I'd not seen it at the time. It was clear to me now. Knowing the truth of Grier's affections allowed me to forgive the year of my life she stole from me.

After all, had it been I that held the key to sending Morna away from me, I couldn't say that I wouldn't have lied, as well. In truth, I knew I would've. There was nothing I wouldn't have done to keep her close to me.

What frightened me was the thought that perhaps Grier felt the same way—that she might still be willing to do anything to keep me close. The power of Morna's magic was pure. Everything she did or sought to do was from a place of love.

Grier had goodness within her, but her purity was buried deep, and her spells didn't always serve the greater good. Her lack of family and the loneliness I suspected she'd experienced most of her life had changed the way she thought of magic. She didn't see her magic as a duty to help. She saw it as a burden that cast her apart. If those around her couldn't accept the magic within her, she would use her powers to force the result she desired.

Grier rarely spoke of her life, but she'd said just enough in our time together to make me understand why she often didn't hesitate to force someone's hand with her magic. The evil she'd had to endure at the hands of frightened, ignorant people over and over throughout her life was enough to send anyone into madness.

I didn't know what I would say to her, but I knew there was a delicate line I would have to balance. My heart could never belong to her, and I had to make sure she understood that. Doing so put me at great risk for upsetting her. If I did—if she believed that I'd somehow betrayed her—there was no telling what Grier might do.

Every step toward my cottage was filled with a silent prayer that all would be well.

I had no confidence it would be.

Morna

The instant I mentioned Grier's name to him, Jerry no longer heard anything else I said. He was distracted, lost in his own thoughts, determined to make his peace with her in whatever way he could.

It pained me to let him go to her, but I knew he was deserving of my trust.

I stood at the edge of the village and watched Jerry walk toward his cottage until I could no longer see him. Once he was out of sight, I took a deep breath. It was time to proceed to the next dreadfully difficult task of the day, breaking my engagement to Henry.

I saw no one on my short walk back to the castle. Inside its walls, Henry was nowhere to be found. Alasdair was the first person I found. He sat relaxing in Father's old chair by the fire. With the room draped in the afternoon's shadow, Alasdair looked so much like Father that my chest squeezed painfully at the sight of him.

"I told everyone they needn't work today. Elspeth and Eoin are abed resting. I couldna sleep."

"Where's Henry? 'Tis time for me to speak to him."

Alasdair shook his head and yawned. Even if he couldn't sleep, he was exhausted.

"He's asleep, as well. Doona wake him just to break his heart. Ye can tell him before dinner."

I didn't argue. While I knew it needed to be done, I was in no hurry to witness his reaction.

"Mayhap, I should wait until morning. Then, he could leave right away should he wish it."

"Ach, he will wish it, lass. No man wants to stay in the home of the lass who has jilted him. Morning then. 'Twill be best..." Alasdair's words slowly faltered as I watched him drift to sleep, his head slumped over against his shoulder.

I must've fallen asleep shortly after, for when my eyes flickered open, Alasdair was gone and only a sliver of sunlight shone into the room.

Evening was upon us, and Jerry would most certainly be wanting to know how everything had gone with Henry.

If I left now, I could reach and return from his cottage before I was expected for dinner.

He wouldn't be pleased, but what was one more evening of waiting when we would have our whole lives to spend together?

If only I'd known how much could change in an evening.

Chapter 33

Jerry

Grier stood in the doorway of my cottage as I approached. While her smile was warm, her eyes were entirely unreadable.

"Did ye know this was my home for many years? 'Tis fitting it should be yer home now."

She gave no greeting and led our conversation with no apology.

"Ye are alive, then?"

"O'course I'm alive. Ye must have known such a fire couldna kill me unless I wished it."

The grief I'd felt at arriving back to see our home destroyed came rushing back to me, flooding my veins with an anger I'd not known I felt toward her.

"I knew no such thing. Do ye not care about the pain ye put me through in the months following what I believed to be yer death? I missed ye, Grier, and the guilt I felt for leaving ye was unbearable."

While my words were true, I realized the moment I said them what a mistake I'd made. Her eyes glistened with hope. My confession made her believe I cared in a way I did not.

"I only meant to help ye. I know Morna has told ye why ye are here. I know that ye know I lied to ye."

Her candor surprised me. I'd expected her to dance around the truth, to spin a tale that would leave me questioning what I knew to be true.

"Aye, I know what ye've done, and I know why."

She stepped inside the cottage as if it were still her home and not mine. I followed her inside. Once the door was closed, she faced me.

"Ye doona know why, lad. How could ye?"

"Ye love me."

Silence didn't bother Grier. She could sit in the company of others surrounded by silence and never feel uncomfortable. I settled into the silence and forced myself to relax inside it as I waited for her to decide how she wished to respond.

"I hope ye know I never intended for things to happen as they did. Ye were not meant for me, and I know it, but ye own my heart anyway."

I couldn't imagine her pain. If I could've eased it, I would have. Had Morna not returned my feelings, it would've killed me. I was doing the same thing to Grier now.

"It honors me to know that ye find me worthy of such affection. Ye are the bonniest friend I've ever known, but aye, I was meant for another, and she holds my heart completely."

The hope in Grier's expression vanished and replaced itself with a cool, collected gaze that made the hairs on the back of my neck stand on end.

"I know, Jerry. Ye needn't tell me where yer heart lies. Ye still canna see, can ye?"

She didn't wait for me to answer before continuing.

"As I told ye, I never intended for things to happen as they have, but they happened all the same. When our home was set aflame, I saw it as my path to redemption, as an opportunity to correct the wrong I did to ye. I intended to stay away, but I could not.

"I lived a life alone and 'twas misery. I canna do it again. I willna do it again. Morna will hate what I've done to her, but she willna be doomed to the same life I've lived. Now that her father is gone, her brother will protect her. He will see that her magic is tended to. He will make certain that her days are never lonely. She will have every chance of having a happy life, and in time she will forget ye."

Panic surged inside me, and I turned to run for the door, all the while knowing it would do no good. I couldn't outrun a spell. I could feel it swirling around me with every step.

"Ye may not love me in the way I wish ye to, but to ye 'twill feel as if ye do. For me, that is better than a life spent alone."

I fought against the pressure in my mind, but I was powerless against her magic. The sound of her words slurred together as my mind went eerily blank.

Morna

I heard sounds coming from Jerry's cottage—primitive, animal-like sounds—but my mind rallied against them. I didn't feel the alarm I should've felt, and I suspected nothing as I knocked on his door.

When no one answered, I pushed it open. As I looked inside, my entire world fell apart.

I should've looked away, but I could not. My brain couldn't believe the sight in front of me.

I'd expected to find Jerry alone.

Grier was still there.

They were wrapped in each other's arms.

With her back pressed against the wall of his cottage, Jerry stood naked before her, driving into her with an abandon that broke my heart. He was entirely unaware of my presence, but Grier saw me the moment I opened the door.

She locked eyes with me, smiled, and threw her head back and laughed.

Chapter 34

Perspective is everything. Seeing Jerry wrapped in Grier's arms should've broken me, but the sudden death of my father had already split me in two. Yes, I was heartbroken. Yes, I was angry. Yes, I felt betrayed, nauseated, and confused. None of it mattered.

The moment Grier laughed, I turned and walked calmly away.

Sometimes life steals the things you love. I wouldn't fight something I couldn't change. I was no match for Grier. Of course Jerry loved her. Every man I'd ever known had. Why would the man who'd spent more time with her than anyone else be any different? He'd been simply biding his time with me until she returned.

I was a fool, and I deserved this betrayal. He'd treated me exactly as I'd treated Henry.

I couldn't move past the pain here. So many horrible things over the course of my still young life held me in chains at Conall Castle. I loved my brother, Elspeth, and Eoin deeply, but the pain was too much. I couldn't stay. Not now.

I shed no tears as I walked back inside the castle. My world was chaos all around me, but inside I felt nothing. I hoped I could hold onto that nothingness forever.

I met Elspeth on the staircase on the way to my bedchamber.

"What's happened, lass? Ye are paler than I've ever seen ye."

I smiled to relieve her worry but quickly stepped into the shadows so she couldn't see my face.

"'Tis nothing. Do ye know where Henry is? I need to speak with him."

"Aye, he's in the dining room with Alasdair."

That was even better. I could tell them both at once.

As was his habit, Alasdair dragged me out of the dining hall to discuss in private what I'd just announced.

I'd never seen him so angry. He was trembling as he held my wrist. I was certain everyone could hear him screaming.

"Have ye lost yer mind, lass? Why would ye tell him ye intend to leave with him tomorrow when we both know ye mean to end yer engagement come morning?"

My insides were like ice. All my life, there was no one who could impact the way I felt more than Alasdair. I cared about his opinion more than anyone. But tonight, his words couldn't break through the wall I'd erected inside.

"My mind is fine. I've decided to keep the engagement. I meant what I told both of ye. I will leave with Henry come morning so we may visit his home and begin preparations for our wedding."

Shaking his head, Alasdair gripped the sides of his head with both hands as he paced wildly in front of me.

"I doona understand a word ye are saying, Morna. I know ye are devastated about Da. I know what it feels like to wish ye could leave here and never step back inside these walls again. The ghost of our memories of him will stay within these walls forever, but we canna run away from this, lass. With time, 'twill get easier."

Calmly, I reached out to touch his arm to stop him.

"This has nothing to do with Father."

"What then? Has Jerry done something to ye? If he's hurt ye lass, I'll kill him."

Even Jerry's name caused me no pain. I was someone who felt everything so intensely. Now I felt nothing. I was beginning to wonder if I'd unintentionally spelled myself.

"Jerry would never hurt me. 'Tis only that he loves another. I dinna see it before, but I see it now. 'Tis time for me to move on from here and live my own life. I shall do so with Henry."

Alasdair shook his head in astonishment. He didn't believe a word I said. I didn't care.

"Love another? Jerry loves none save ye. Everyone sees the way he looks at ye. What has gotten into ye, lass? Ye have me worried."

"Grier is back, Alasdair, and Jerry loves her. I saw the two of them together."

Alasdair jerked back as if I'd slapped him.

"Grier? Why dinna ye tell me that first? We both know she is up to no good. We've known that ever since Jerry arrived here. Ye canna trust her."

"Aye, I know, and now I canna trust Jerry either. I wish to leave here. Will ye allow me to do so? Ye told me once that if ye were laird ye would let me be the woman I wished. Ye are laird now. Will ye keep yer word?"

It was a cruel way for me to persuade him to allow me to make my own decisions. Just like Father, Alasdair's word meant everything to him.

"O'course, I'll permit ye, but I doona care for it for so many reasons. Jerry aside, lass, 'tis not proper for ye to travel with a man ye are not yet wed to without an escort, and I willna leave Elspeth while she is with child. MacNeal Castle is verra far from here. If trouble came to ye, there is no guarantee I could reach ye in time."

I no longer had any concern for my own wellbeing. It was as frozen as every other emotion inside me. "No harm will befall me, and Mary and Kip can stay until we are wed. Would that suit ye?"

It was a ridiculous suggestion by societal expectations, but Alasdair had never much cared about what anyone else thought. As long as someone he trusted was there to watch over me, that was all he cared about.

Reluctantly, he nodded.

"Aye, I suppose 'twill do. Ye do know ye doona have to marry him, lass. If ye doona love him, I wish ye would not. Ye can still send him away and live here until another ye could love crosses yer path. Ye are always welcome here. And ye needn't worry about the pain Jerry may cause ye. I shall banish the two of them from this territory come morning, and ye shall never see them again."

I knew I didn't have to marry, that Alasdair would take care of me until his dying day if I wished it, but Alasdair had his own family to tend to, and it was time for me to go out on my own.

"Aye, banish them, but it will change nothing. I've agreed to marry Henry, and I willna go back on my word."

Alasdair's arms wrapped around and lifted me into the air as he hugged me. His words were choked and broken as he spoke. Although I couldn't see his eyes, I knew he was crying.

"This is a mistake, lass. The moment ye realize it, please know ye can come home. There is nothing ye can ever do that will make that impossible. Whatever happens, know that I will protect ye here."

He clung to me desperately as I hung limply in his arms. I didn't fight his embrace, but I didn't hug him back, either.

"Do ye wish me to kill him, lass? 'Twould be a horrible sin, but I will do it if ye wish it."

What frightened me more than anything else I'd witnessed all day was how long it took me to answer him.

"No, but thank ye."

The realization that I'd even considered it told me just how much of me was truly gone—locked beneath a fortress I had no desire to unearth.

Chapter 35

Come morning, as we packed and loaded everything onto a dozen different horses, Jerry was absent from the stables. Without a word to end things, he'd left me for Grier.

Mary approached me tenderly, placing a hand on my back as she spoke in soft tones. She was furious at everyone—at Jerry for what he'd done, at Alasdair for letting me leave, at Kip for agreeing that they would come with me—but she was treating me with unnecessary kindness.

"Ye left the dress ye wore yesterday out of yer belongings, but I added it to yer chests, so ye needn't worry. 'Twill all get better, lass. With time, everything will be better."

"I know, Mary. I'm fine. Truly. Go and scream at Alasdair and Kip if ye wish it. Once we leave, ye willna be able to."

She looked at me with the same concerned gaze Alasdair had given me the day before, but I turned away and ignored it until she left.

There were only two people who occupied my mind—two people who even with my frozen emotions, I would be desperately sad to leave—Eoin and Elspeth.

Eoin threatened to break through my resolve most of all. The poor lad was already so saddened and confused from his grandfather's death that I worried what my sudden absence might do to him. I wanted him to be certain he would see me again.

I found him on the floor of his bedchamber stacking small stones he'd gathered from the woods into piles.

"Eoin, lad, do ye mind if I join ye?"

He smiled and waved me to the floor with his chubby little hand. As I sat next to him, he pushed a few rocks in my direction.

"Da found them."

"Oh, yer da found the rocks, did he? Did ye help him?"

He nodded, but said nothing else. He was unusually quiet.

"Eoin, did yer da tell ye that I must leave here for awhile?"

He kept his head down, fumbling with the rocks on the floor. His voice was soft and sad when he spoke.

"Will ye leave like Grand Da?"

A lump swelled in my throat, and I hurried to lift Eoin from the floor and into my lap before every emotion I was holding inside broke loose in front of him.

"No, lad. I'll never leave like Grand Da. I'll only be away for a time, and then ye will see me. I shall visit ye here. Mayhap ye can come and visit me at my new castle."

Simply knowing he would see me again seemed to relax him, and he lay his little head against my chest as I held him. With every person in the castle dealing with grief over my father's death and Elspeth dealing with the exhaustion of her pregnancy, little Eoin had been left to fend for himself more than he was accustomed.

When he began to snore, I carefully stood and carried him to his bed. Kissing his brow, I whispered a spell of protection in his ear and bid him farewell.

Elspeth was even more upset by my decision than Alasdair. Never one to mince words, Elspeth rained a stream of curse words down on me that I wouldn't have thought her capable of.

"Ye are a selfish wee bitch, Morna. I doona wish to see ye. I doona wish to say goodbye to ye. Ye can burn in hell for all I care."

Undeterred by her rage, I moved across the room and climbed onto the bed next to her where she sat resting.

"Ye needn't be angry with me. Ye should be pleased that I'm leaving. Ye know Alasdair worries too much for me. Ye and Eoin should be his priority."

She screamed at me between sobs. Her eyes were bloodshot, and she dabbed at her nose with a cloth.

"Do ye think Alasdair is the only one in this damned castle who cares for ye? What will Eoin do? His heart has already been broken once this week. And what of the new babe? Do ye have no desire to know it, to love it as ye have loved Eoin? And what of me, Morna? I know I am not yer closest friend, but ye know ye are mine. I doona care what Jerry has done to ye. 'Tis selfish of ye to do this, and 'tis pure lunacy for ye to marry a man like Henry MacNeal."

So what if Henry could be unkind? I could be unkind, too. So what if he hid something? I was hiding something from him, as well. Everyone seemed so much more concerned about my fiancé than I was.

"Elspeth, I canna stay here. Ye wouldna stay here if ye were me. I know ye wouldna. Ye would want yer own life, with yer own family. Is it so wrong for me to desire to have just what ye do?"

She collapsed into a hysterical fit of tears. As I moved in to comfort her, she turned her swollen eyes up toward me.

"O'course 'tisn't wrong. 'Tis only that I will miss ye so much I doona know if I can bear it. I wish ye would be here for the birth, Morna. I've not said a word to Alasdair, but I'm frightened. So verra frightened."

I pulled back to look at her more fully. Her confession alarmed me.

"What do ye mean? Do ye feel as if something is wrong with the babe?"

She continued to cry as she spoke, and I pulled her in close to stroke her hair.

"No, the babe feels strong, but I feel weak. I doona have the same strength I had when carrying Eoin."

I tried to rationalize her worry.

"Ye are older now. 'Tis no wonder that ye doona feel as strong. All will be well, I'm sure of it."

Elspeth pulled away from me and turned to grasp my hand. She squeezed my fingers so tightly I couldn't help but devote every ounce of my attention to listening to her.

"Ye must hear me, Morna. I doona believe I will survive the child's birth. Where will Alasdair and Eoin be if we both leave them?"

"What?" Horror washed over me making me dizzy at Elspeth's suggestion. It was absurd for her to even allow herself to think it. I pulled my hand away and grabbed her shoulders, shaking them gently as I yelled at her. "Doona say anything like that again, Elspeth."

"My denying it will help nothing. Yer father knew, ye know? He knew that death was coming for him."

Glimpses of him tucking me into bed flickered through my mind. I knew Elspeth was right—he'd suspected he would be gone soon, and he wanted to make his peace with me before he was.

"What does Father have to do with any of this?"

"I know how he felt because I feel it now, and ye are the only one I mean to tell. Ye must promise me not to tell Alasdair."

Just like with the news of her pregnancy, there was no reason for her to feel the need to ask me not to say anything to him. I would do anything to keep my brother from pain. There was no way Elspeth could possibly know for certain she would die in childbirth, and I wouldn't worry my brother over something that would very likely turn out to be irrelevant.

"O'course, Elspeth, but ye must not give in to this feeling ye have. Ye must try to stay strong. We all need ye."

Tears fell freely down her face. She was still so stunning that I found myself jealous of her even with her face splotched red.

"I know ye feel ye must go now, but will ye try to be back for the birth in three months' time? If I am to die, ye will need to be here for Alasdair's sake. He can bear so much, but this would test him in a way I doona believe he's prepared for."

I would go to MacNeal Castle and make preparations for my wedding, but there was no way I would possibly miss the babe's birth now.

"I'll be back in two, Elspeth, and all will be well. Ye will see."

Chapter 36

"Did ye not wish to say goodbye to Jerry, lass? I know the two of ye were verra good friends."

Henry asked the question two days into our ride, catching me off guard and forcing me out of the silence I'd enjoyed for the entirety of our trip.

I shook my head but kept my gaze ahead. "We were not so verra close."

"'Tis no matter." Henry paused, and I could see him looking at me expectantly out of the corner of my eye.

"Why is that?"

"He will be joining us in a fortnight. I heard that yer brother no longer required his services so I asked if he wished to work for me at MacNeal Castle. He agreed as long as his sister could live with him."

Mary snorted behind me. While I worked hard to remain emotionless, this sudden news nearly caused me to fall off my horse.

Whirling my head toward him, my voice gave too much away. "He what? He's coming to work as yer servant?"

Henry nodded, and I noticed that his expression was rather furious. I wondered if he'd heard rumors about Jerry and me and my reaction had only confirmed them in his mind.

"Aye, lass. He and his sister."

I couldn't stop myself. The words ground their way through my teeth against my will.

"She is not his sister."

Henry waved a hand dismissively as if he already knew that.

"In truth, I doona care what she is to him. I see no reason to judge a man for how he lives his life in private as long as he does good work for me. I watched Jerry at yer brother's home, and he is a fair worker. I canna imagine why Alasdair saw a need to get rid of him."

His tone was accusatory. I saw no need to escalate the situation further.

"How many days until we reach home?"

I intentionally refrained from labeling MacNeal Castle as only his home. I hoped my inclusive wording of the question would cause him to relax.

"Less than a day. We shall arrive by nightfall."

There was a loud stirring in the trees to our left. Henry halted the horses as we waited for the animal within the brush to either retreat or step into the pathway in front of us. I expected a deer. Instead a tall, strapping highlander tripped his way in front of Henry's horse.

"*Pretend ye know me, lass. Otherwise, this lad will send me away, and I must speak with ye.*"

I heard the stranger's voice inside my mind as clearly as if he'd said the words aloud, but his lips never moved. The sudden intrusion inside my mind startled me so much that this time, I did fall off my horse. Before I could stand, the stranger's hands were on my arms, gently lifting me from the ground.

"Remove yer hands from my betrothed, sir." Henry's voice screamed as he dismounted and made his way over to us. "Morna, are ye all right, lass? What happened? Did ye faint?"

The stranger kept his grip on my arms and spoke quickly inside my mind once again.

"*Did ye hear me? Ye must hurry. Throw yer arms around me and greet me as if ye've known me all yer life. Ye can call me Hamish. Tell him I'm a cousin and insist that I come with ye.*"

Too shocked and baffled to argue, I did exactly what the man asked of me. Throwing my arms around him, squeezing him with an intimacy that surprised even me, I gushed out loud about this man I'd never before seen in my life.

"Hamish! What are ye doing here? What fortune that our paths have crossed? Ye must join us. We are not far from home now, and ye look bone weary from travel."

Surprising myself more with each passing moment, I twisted with one arm still around Hamish as I turned to address Henry.

"Ye doona mind if he stays at the castle, do ye? This is my cousin, Hamish Conall, my father's brother's son."

Henry was caught off guard, but he could hardly refuse to shelter a relative of the woman he meant to marry, and I knew it.

Masking his frustration, Henry nodded and extended the man his hand.

"O'course. Do ye have no horse? Where were ye headed when ye crossed our path?"

For the first time since his sudden intrusion, Hamish spoke out loud. His voice sounded exactly like it did inside my mind.

"No, I'm afraid my horse was stolen from me. 'Tis indeed great fortune that I stumbled upon ye, for 'twas my cousin's home where I was headed."

Mary's bugged-out eyes caught my attention, and I discreetly shook my head to warn her to say nothing.

"I see. Well, we've an extra horse with no baggage. Ye can ride her, though she's slower than the rest. Ye will have to take up the rear."

Hamish happily agreed. Once he saw himself mounted, our caravan of travelers continued. The moment all was quiet, Hamish's voice spoke to me in my mind once again.

"Ye can speak back to me in yer mind, lass. I'm surprised ye havena even tried."

I was too confused for it to have even crossed my mind. Hesitantly, I attempted to think what I wished to say out loud to him.

"What are ye?"

"I'm the same as ye, lass. I possess magic, and I felt yers vibrating through the forest from far away. I've been trying to meet up with ye for days."

This man wasn't the same as me. If he was powerful enough to communicate with me in such a way, he possessed more power than I'd known was possible.

"Where are ye from? And why were ye trying to meet me?"

238

"I make it a point to speak with everyone I meet like us, lass, though we are scattered few and far between. I'm from Allen territory, Morna. I believe yer brother sent someone after me many months ago. I'm sorry it has taken me so long to find ye."

The druid Alasdair sought, the one he believed could teach me everything I needed to know about magic, was here.

Suddenly, the darkness of the past week seemed a little bit brighter.

Chapter 37

MacNeal Castle—Two Weeks Later

It took less than a day of settling into his own territory, in his own home, around his own servants for me to see exactly what everyone warned me about Henry MacNeal. The man was an arrogant brute who thought himself better than anyone below his station. He was disingenuous in everything he said, and I suspected that his tendency toward violence was something he struggled to restrain daily.

If not for Hamish's presence at the castle, I would've fled with Mary and Kip the day after we arrived. But the one positive thing about being in Henry's home was that I rarely saw him.

He never visited my room, he hadn't touched me since we arrived, and his days were spent tending to tasks left unattended while he was at Conall Castle.

It meant that I had the castle, or at least the rooms he'd given me, entirely to myself. I spent my days with Hamish. He taught me more in the span of a fortnight than I'd learned in the past decade.

The lessons were a glorious distraction from so many things I didn't want to think about. Unfortunately, Hamish didn't allow me to stay in bliss for long. On the day Jerry and Grier were set to arrive at the castle, the mysterious druid told me he was leaving.

"Must ye go? I could spend years working with ye and not learn all that I wish to."

"Aye I must, lass, though leaving ye 'twill sadden me more than ye know. If I dinna already know yer heart belonged to another, I would've spent the past fortnight trying to earn yer heart rather than improving yer spells."

I could never tell when Hamish was teasing me—he so often said things I found surprising. I'd never mentioned Jerry to him, and I suspected he knew the truth of my feelings for Henry.

"Just who do ye think my heart belongs to?"

He shrugged in a way that only accentuated the length of his arms.

"I doona know, but I know 'tis not Laird MacNeal."

I didn't want to speak about Jerry. I only wanted to beg Hamish to stay.

"Please doona leave. I need ye. I went too long without someone to teach me."

Dropping to his knees, Hamish situated himself on the floor and patted the ground so that I would join him.

"I must leave, but I will always be willing to teach ye. Ye are welcome in Allen territory any time. Those with magic are safe there, and our practice is looked at in a verra different way. Ye would like it."

Perhaps I would follow him. Once I ended my engagement for good and Elspeth's babe was safely delivered, I could go to Allen territory and devote myself to a life of learning. There were many other possible futures that seemed much worse to me.

"Do ye mean it? I will come then. There are things I must see to first, but later, I will come."

Hamish smiled and nodded.

"'Tis settled then. I shall count the days until I see ye again."

I laughed, again unsure if his small flirtations were genuine or meant in jest.

"How far is yer home from here?"

"'Tis closer from here than 'tis from Conall Castle. Though in truth, 'tis not all that far from Conall Castle either."

I thought of the months Jerry had been away while searching for him. It had to be further than Hamish realized.

"It took a man I knew weeks to reach the village when he went in search of ye. How is that not too far?"

"'Tis our magic. The forest surrounding us is spelled. Unless we know ye are coming and can clear the path for ye, anyone searching will have a verra difficult time finding us. 'Tis a wonder the lad ever found it. This lad ye speak of—is he the one who holds yer heart?"

"No one holds my heart, Hamish."

"Aye, someone does. For if not, ye would belong to me by now. Did ye know, lass, that if I were to say four simple words, I would break the spell ye've cast on yerself and ye would fall to pieces here in my arms? There is a pain inside ye that ye have buried so deep 'twill poison ye. I understand what 'tis to hurt, lass, but hiding from how ye feel only keeps ye blind."

While the thought had crossed my mind the day I found Jerry and Grier together, I'd not truly thought it possible. Had my feelings truly been so overwhelming in that moment that I'd cast a spell on myself unwittingly?

"Do ye mean I've a spell on me in a literal or figurative sense, Hamish?"

He smiled. "Literal, lass. Quite a powerful one. Do ye wish me to break it?"

Bracing for the pain I knew would come, I nodded.

Rather than the breaking of a dam, it was like a slow trickle of rain. The feelings came in a slow steady stream. As Hamish opened his arms to me, I leaned into him and told him everything.

By nightfall, Hamish was gone. While a sense of misery hung over me with such intensity that I had to remind myself to breathe under the weight of it, I was grateful that I felt like myself for the first time in weeks.

I could see things clearly. I knew what I had to do.

I couldn't marry Henry. And I had to find out if Hamish was right. His last words to me would haunt me until I did.

"The lad still holds yer heart, lass. If he truly loved her, 'twould have been released back to ye. I suspect she's spelled him. The only way for ye to know for certain is to get him far away from her and see if he begins to wage a war within himself. If he is spelled, he canna do so while near her."

Chapter 38

M ary and I created a plan, albeit a faulty one, in the little time I had before dinner.

I would extend my meal with Henry for as long as possible. While he was eating and distracted, Mary and Kip would ready our horses. We both knew that once the engagement was broken, it would be in our best interest to leave MacNeal Castle with haste.

In the meantime, I simply needed to pack all of my things and have them ready to be loaded before dinner.

With everything folded, I bent to my knees to put everything away.

Jerry's letter fell to the floor from the folded clothes the moment I opened my chest. I'd not thought of it once since he'd given it to me weeks ago.

Sinking to the floor, I opened it with shaking hands.

My dearest Morna,

Oh, how I wish our first night together had not ended in such tragedy for you. There were so many things I wished to tell you that next morning, so many ways I wished to show you just how much I treasure your heart.

These past days have been a misery for me. You should not have to go through such grief alone, though I understand why your brother has asked me to stay away.

Lass, I know you worry that you are somehow responsible for pulling me from my own time. It is a waste of time. I don't care who brought me here, I am only glad to have arrived.

Do you know how many times since meeting you I've looked up into the stars and pondered how I could have been so lucky? More times than I can count.

I'm an ordinary lad who until vanishing through time lived a very ordinary life.

You have made my life spectacular. And you have done the impossible. You made me love you more than I love myself, and we both know that I love myself a great deal.

I hope you know what you've gotten yourself into, lass, for even if you were to wish it now, I'm afraid you're stuck with me. You possess my very soul—you stole it the moment I laid eyes on you.

There is naught in this world I wouldn't do for you.

All my love,

Jerry

Only someone who was exceedingly cruel would take the time to give someone such a letter if they intended to leave them the very same day. Jerry was anything but cruel.

246

Our plan went disastrously wrong from the start. I arrived at dinner to learn that Henry had chosen to skip it. Panicked that he might see Kip and Mary readying our things and take preventative actions to keep me from leaving, I went in search of him.

It didn't take long. Only a few steps outside the dining hall, I could hear Henry screaming at someone. His tone was angry and violent. I hurried in its direction to see what was happening. He was in one of the castle's four main towers, and I ran up the steps.

The charming, seductive man I knew was unrecognizable as he stared down at a girl younger than me who stood shaking before him.

I didn't know what she'd done to upset him, but the moment I stepped into the circular room, he slapped her. Without hesitation, I launched myself between them, pushing him away as I ushered the girl from the tower, whispering in her ear for her to run.

When I faced Henry, his face had drained of color. He preferred to lose his temper in private, when no one was watching. He believed this was the first sign of it I'd seen, and he was visibly embarrassed for being caught.

He attempted to give an explanation, but I held up a hand to interrupt him.

"No, it doesna matter what the lass did to ye, 'twas no reason to hit her."

Glancing down, he pretended to be regretful.

247

"Ye are right. The stress of all the work that awaited me when I returned here wears on me. I shouldna have lost my temper."

I was so angry that the sole reason for finding him was no longer at the forefront of my mind.

"From what I've heard, 'tis not the first time ye've lost yer temper with a servant."

His left brow twitched ever so slightly—a small flash of anger that he masked quickly.

"Have my servants been speaking to ye, lass? They know they are to leave ye be unless ye require them."

"'Twas not anyone here, though I suspect they are all too terrified of ye to say anything. 'Twas friends from Conall Castle. No one thought I should come here with ye."

He seemed to be searching for someone to blame—someone he could take his anger out on.

"'Twas Kip, then. Aye, I yelled at the lad once. He deserved it. I was verra clear on which stall I wished for my horse to stay in. He disobeyed me."

I could feel the magic begin to twitch within my fingertips. Even with only two weeks of training, my powers were more integrated into my being. It took little for me to call on them now, and my anger had it at the ready.

"Kip doesna take orders from ye. Not at Conall Castle and not here. I am sorry to break my word to ye Henry, but I canna marry ye."

He laughed and stepped forward to pin me against the wall.

"I've tried to be patient with ye, lass, but ye have overstepped. Ye are in my home. I shall treat my servants however I wish, and I doona allow anyone to break their word to me."

"The man I see before me now is not the man I agreed to marry. I'm under no obligation to stay here. My brother will welcome me back with open arms. My horses are ready. I plan to leave at once."

For a moment, I thought he would step away, that things would end peacefully, but as the silence stretched, I watched him change his mind. One moment, his palms braced the wall on either side of my head, the next his hands were on my waist, squeezing as he pushed me into the stones so hard that I feared my ribs would break.

He leaned in close, and the warm breath that once threatened to seduce me now made my skin crawl.

"Ye bedded him, dinna ye, lass—the stable hand? I heard talk of it and still I was willing to wed ye. Ye dare chastise me for my anger when I have treated ye with nothing but respect. I believed ye to be the kind of lass who would go to her marriage pure. Had I known ye were a whore, I would've bedded ye myself long ago. Mayhap 'tis time for me to do so now."

I had hoped to leave MacNeal Castle without revealing my powers to a man undeserving of the knowledge, but the moment his hand grabbed at the center between my legs, I let go of any apprehension I had about spelling him.

My first instinct, however, wasn't to utter a spell. In my haste to get his hands off me, I did the only thing that came to mind. I lifted one hand in the air and jabbed two fingers so deeply into his eyes that I swore I heard one of them pop. He fell back screaming and gasping as blood poured from his eyes.

"My eyes! I canna see. I canna see."

249

He screamed the words over and over as I retched onto the ground.

I couldn't imagine the pain he was in, but I suspected I'd not blinded him permanently. His rage gave him the strength to stand. Just as he tried to charge me, I spoke a spell that bound him against the wall, making him unable to move anything other than his mouth.

I stood back and watched him as he realized what I was.

"Ye are a witch. I dinna believe the rumors. Had I known, I never would've agreed to marry ye."

It was oddly satisfying to watch him panic at the knowledge—knowing that he could do nothing to prevent anything I wished to do to him. I stayed silent as he rambled on.

"Do ye mean to kill me? Would ye kill a man for losing his temper?"

I wondered if perhaps I should, but I knew that I could not. While the world would most certainly be a better place without him, I couldn't live with blood on my hands.

"No, I willna kill ye, but if ye ever slap one of yer servants again or if ye ever try to bed a lass against her will, rest assured I will learn of it. When I do, I shall come and cut yer tongue out while ye sleep."

The admittance that I wouldn't kill him made him bold.

"Witchcraft is an offense punishable by death, lass. When I am free, I will let all of the Highlands know what ye are. Then even yer dear brother will be unable to help ye."

The spell wouldn't hold him forever. I wasn't even sure I would have enough time to get Jerry away from Grier before Henry was free of my spell. There was no sense in arguing with him further. I wouldn't kill him, and he knew it.

"I could always cut yer tongue out now, then ye would be unable to tell anyone anything ever again."

I hated that I wasn't as frightening as I wanted to be. He easily called my bluff.

"Ye retched after poking my eyes. Ye doona have the nerve to cut out my tongue."

Placing both hands on his shoulders, I smiled.

"Ye are right. Goodbye, Henry."

Swinging my knee far back behind me, I threw it into his groin with so much force that I knew it was he that would now be retching long after I left.

Chapter 39

I ran from the tower as quickly as my feet could carry me. I didn't stop until I burst into the stables, screaming for Mary and Kip to meet me.

They were ready with all of our belongings, though we'd had no opportunity to plan how best to get Jerry alone.

I'd not seen him since the day I walked in on he and Grier in his cottage. I wasn't sure my already rattled nerves could take it.

"Ye must breathe, lass. We've still much to do. We must do it quickly. Kip has a plan."

More surprised than was perhaps appropriate, I lifted my eyes to look at him. Kip was a man of few words. To think he'd been sitting around thinking of a way to help me touched me deeply.

"Ye've a plan, Kip? Whatever 'tis I'm willing to try it. I'm too shaken to think."

Kip's calm demeanor helped ease my breathing as he approached and placed a gentle hand on my shoulder.

"Ye look it, lass. How did MacNeal react?"

Still trying to catch my breath, I spoke in broken lengths.

"Not well...he...he knows I'm a witch...and I might...I might have blinded him. I canna say for sure."

"Well, lass," his voice still calm and steady, Kip continued on like there was nothing unusual about what I'd just told him, "we best get started then before he has a chance to send his men after us. Here is what I propose:

"Under no circumstance can Grier see ye. She willna trust ye and will hide Jerry away. I doona trust Mary to approach her. She's too angry and willna be able to hide it. I must be the one to lead Grier away from their new home in the village, and I know just how to do it."

We approached the dimly lit home as quietly as we could, tying one horse just a short distance away while the rest remained tied in the woods for our escape. Mary and I sat on the ground on the left side of the cottage, our backs pressed against the wall.

The moment we saw Kip leave with Grier, we would enter and try to speak with Jerry. At that point, the result of our efforts was entirely dependent upon his reaction.

The cottage was in terrible condition, but its thin walls allowed us to hear every word as Kip burst inside without knocking.

"Grier, ye've arrived just in time. I need yer help most urgently."

I wanted to scream in response to the rage that built inside me at the sound of Grier's voice, but her tone echoed surprise, and it gave me hope that Kip's plan just might work.

"What's happened?"

"'Tis Laird MacNeal. He's been attacked by one of his servants and tied up in a tower. I canna stop his bleeding."

"Have ye called for a healer?"

Kip played his part wonderfully. His voice never faltered, and his story never slipped as she questioned him.

"There is no time for that, lass. Only magic will save him, and Morna doesna possess the skills to aid him. If ye are worried that someone will learn of yer magic, ye needn't be. I killed the servant that harmed him. Only Morna is with him now."

I could hear Grier gathering things inside, and Mary reached over to squeeze my hand. Whispering so quietly that it was barely above a breath, Mary spoke, "'Tis almost time. Are ye ready to see him?"

"No, but as long as ye are by my side, I will be fine."

From inside, I heard Jerry's voice for the first time. "Do ye need me to go with ye?"

"No." There was such command in the way she said it that I knew Jerry would object to her ordering him around. His silence was all the proof I needed that something was terribly wrong with him. "Which tower is he in, Kip?"

"The west tower. I'll lead ye there."

"No, ye stay here with Jerry. Ye would only slow me down if ye came. Doona leave here until I return."

I held my breath as I watched her leave. Once Kip believed it safe, he called us inside.

It would've been so much easier if he'd looked different—if his eyes appeared spelled or if he'd not recognized me. What made it so much more painful was that he looked exactly the same, and he knew who I was immediately. He simply didn't care.

"Morna, Mary, what are ye doing here? Ye should have entered with Kip. I'm sure Grier would've loved to have seen ye."

It was such a ridiculous question—a ridiculous statement—I couldn't even bring myself to respond to him.

Fortunately, Mary found herself far less speechless than I. She marched right over to him and grabbed his head between both of her hands.

"Ye listen to me, ye damned fool. What is the matter with ye? How can ye speak to her so plainly after what ye've done to her? Doona ye remember that ye love her?"

"Morna?"

The confusion in Jerry's voice sounded entirely genuine.

Mary shook him a little more violently than was necessary.

"Aye, Morna. O'course Morna. Do ye really mean to tell me ye doona remember loving her?"

Understandably, Jerry pulled away from her. As he approached, my entire body went still.

"What is she going on about, lass? I did love ye, but I love ye no longer. I thought everyone knew by now."

Nothing could've wounded me more. He remembered everything. She'd simply changed his feelings entirely.

Kip was in no mood to dawdle. He knew it would take Grier no time to realize she'd been tricked.

"I doona believe the castle is enough distance, lass. We must take him with us."

Before any of us could respond, Kip lifted a candlestick and struck Jerry on the back of the head.

Chapter 40

J erry was a docile captive. He didn't scream or thrash about once he gained consciousness. Instead, he told us repeatedly, as Kip secured the bindings keeping him strapped belly-down on my horse, that whatever we were trying to do to him was futile—that Grier would be along soon and would find him.

We all knew he was right. The first place Grier would go was Conall Castle. She would try to find us on the path. I couldn't go that direction with him.

"I doona know where Allen territory is, but 'twould be best if I took Jerry there. Grier knows nothing of Hamish. The two of ye should come with me, as well. I hate to think what Grier might do to ye once she catches up with ye."

Mary wasn't worried.

"We must return to Conall Castle. Alasdair must know what's happened so he may decide how to prepare for it before hearing of it elsewhere. If that bitch comes for us, I'll run her through."

Jerry started to protest at Mary's description of Grier, but Mary just slapped the top of his head to shush him.

"No, doona ye say another word about her, Jerry. I doona wish to hear it and neither does Morna." She twisted to address me. "Morna, did ye learn anything with Hamish that might give us more time—that might make us less catchable?"

It was a simple enough spell but one I doubted Grier would expect me to know. It was much like what his clan used to keep their territory hidden.

"Aye, I'll muddy yer path a bit. Ride ahead, and once I canna see ye, I'll cast it."

They didn't waste any time, and as they reached the edge of the village, Kip called back after me. "Hamish left towards the east, lass. Mayhap, if ye ride quickly enough ye can catch him."

With Jerry draped over the back of my horse like a blanket, I climbed in front of him and took off as quickly as possible in an eastwardly direction.

I didn't stop at all the first night. I cast a spell to light our path and continued through the woods, hoping with each passing second we would meet up with Hamish. He was nowhere to be found, and the mind-speak that had been available to me the day he stumbled across our path wasn't working either.

All I had was a few blankets to see us through to Allen territory.

"Lass, is there truly any reason for this? Ye are my friend, Morna, but this willna work. Ye canna force me to love ye."

He'd said little since we left. I was so concerned with trying to sense whether or not we were traveling in the right direction I'd almost forgotten about him.

"Oh, really? Ye do know that is precisely what Grier has done to ye, aye? Stolen ye from me and forced ye to love her? Yer feelings for her are not real, Jerry. She's spelled ye."

He was quick to protest. "No. Grier wouldna ever spell me."

"Doona be a fool. Even if ye feel as if ye love her now, 'tis clear enough ye still have yer mind. Ye know how ruthless and vengeful she can be. Do ye truly believe that if she were hurt enough, she wouldna spell anyone to make them do anything she wanted?"

He fell silent for a long time, and I knew he believed it possible. Just as the sun began to break along the horizon, he spoke again.

"Is it truly necessary to keep me bound this way? All my blood has run to my head. 'Tis causing me to feel rather ill, and my head aches dreadfully."

"We will stop and rest soon. As long as ye promise to cause me no trouble, I'll allow ye to ride properly when we continue."

True to my word, as soon as the sun was up, I found a place to rest.

"All right Jerry, I'm going to help ye to yer feet. Ye may be unsteady for a moment."

Untying him, I pushed him off the horse so that his feet landed first. He held onto the horse for a brief moment then took off running in the opposite direction.

Sighing, I muttered a spell to trip him and watched while his legs locked, and he fell flat on his face. He only made it a few strides away.

"Doona ye remember I'm a witch, too?"

With his head still down, it took him some effort to answer me. "Aye, but ye are not a verra good one. I thought mayhap I could get away."

Moving to stand in front of him, I nudged his shoulders so he would lift his head.

Begrudgingly, he did so. Blood was running freely down the front of his face.

"Ye cracked my skull open, lass. Do ye know of a spell that might heal it?"

It looked worse than it was, but the sight of him losing so much blood had me in tears as I led him to the river to clean his wound. I knew of nothing that would heal the wound completely. As long as we held something to it, I knew it would stop bleeding soon. I was far more upset by it than Jerry was.

"'Tis all right, lass. 'Twas my own fault for trying to run."

He'd removed his shirt so I could clean the wound with it. Wetting it, I reached up to wipe more blood from his face.

"Are ye truly so eager to get away from me? Ye've said ye remember our time together. How then can ye be so callous about it?"

He closed his eyes as I pressed the cloth against his wound.

"I doona know, lass. I can only tell ye how I feel. I remember loving ye, but I canna feel the memory of it. I can only see it in my mind. I know I dinna mean to hurt ye, but when I think of Grier, all I feel is this overwhelming love and concern for her. That is why I tried to run. I know she's worried for me, and I canna stand the thought of her in pain."

"Ye felt just as strongly for me a fortnight ago. Can ye truly not see that ye might be spelled? How could yer feelings change so quickly otherwise?"

With his face now clean and the crack above his brow clotting nicely, he looked up into my eyes and stared at me in silence for a long time.

When he smiled, my heart fluttered with hope.

"Mayhap, I am, lass. Why doona ye kiss me, and we shall see how I feel?"

I'd missed the feeling of his lips so much that I threw myself into the kiss with abandon. It felt as if he were back. His hands caressed the sides of my face, his lips moved against mine willingly, his tongue slipped deftly inside. For me, it was perfect, but when it ended, Jerry leaned casually back and shrugged his shoulders.

"Nothing, lass. I felt nothing."

Just as I was about to collapse into a heap of embarrassed tears, Hamish's voice approached us from behind.

"Ach, lass. There is not a man alive that could be kissed like that and feel nothing. She's spelled him worse than I thought."

Chapter 41

<u>Note from M.C.:</u>

How are you doing, lass? I trust you are still reading and eager to hear how things turn out in the end. As I mentioned to you before, it's important for you to hear my story—it will make everything easier for you to believe once we meet.

While I know you may have your doubts about the reality of everything now, one way I can assure you my story is true is this: Were this a work of fiction, I most assuredly would not have written these next two chapters of my life.

My father's death was difficult to bear.

My own death was so much worse.

Allen Territory—One Month Later

“ **I** should have never told ye about this place, lass. Either way, regardless of what ye see within that pool, only pain can come from it. Please let me take ye back to the village. My uncle will continue to work with Jerry. Not a soul here will allow him to leave, and if Grier comes for him, ye know her magic is no match for what we have here. I'll come with ye to Conall Castle. We'll stay for the babe's birth and learn what shall happen as everyone is meant to. 'Tis never a good thing to know another's future."

Hamish's warning was useless. I'd made up my mind the moment he mentioned it. I couldn't stand the unknown for a moment longer. Everything in my life felt as if it were one day away from entire destruction. If the waters within Hamish's cave would allow me to know one way or the other how things would play out, then I wanted to know. I was in pain anyway. How much worse could it get?

"Just tell me how it works, Hamish. Please. If Elspeth's worry is for naught, I willna leave Jerry here. If she has truly predicted her death, we shall go and leave Jerry in yer uncle's care."

Grier's spell still held Jerry with a tight grip, and in the weeks since our arrival, he'd grown angry and cold. He hated me now. The way he looked at me sent shivers down my spine each and every time—his eyes were filled with malice.

"'Twill only show ye things that are unchangeable, which is precisely why it causes such pain. No matter what horrible things ye find inside, ye can do nothing to stop them."

I was quickly losing my patience with him. "I doona care if I canna change them. At least I will know and can make my peace with whatever is inside."

Hamish shook his head but turned to leave.

"Verra well. I'll wait for ye outside."

I don't know how long I cried on the wet stones surrounding the shallow pool, but Hamish eventually gave up waiting and came inside to collect me. He picked me up in his long, broad arms and cradled me like a child.

"What did ye see, lass?"

"Elspeth will die, and then, so will I."

Hamish's arms seized uncomfortably at my words. He dropped me to my feet and held me out away from him.

"What?"

I repeated the words slowly, terror gripping at me even as I said them. I didn't want to die. Not yet. There was still so much I wanted, so much I still needed to do.

"Elspeth…she was right. She dies giving birth to a beautiful baby boy. One month later, Alasdair will bury me, as well."

The expression on Hamish's face surprised me. He didn't look devastated by the revelation, and I started to believe that every flattering comment, every sideways glance had been in jest. If anything, he just looked confused.

"Did ye see yerself die? What killed ye?"

Sniffling between sobs, I screamed at him. "What does it matter how I die? Does it not bother ye to know I'll be dead in a few weeks?"

Hamish brushed the wet and matted hair from my face and bent forward to kiss my cheek. "Lass, ye dinna see yerself die, did ye?"

I shook my head. "No, I only saw my lifeless body being lowered into the ground."

He smiled and rubbed his hands up and down my arms to warm me.

"If ye dinna see yerself die, if ye dinna see what killed ye, then ye willna die. Did no one ever tell ye that witches doona die like everyone else? Unless harmed by the magic of another, 'tis up to us when our life ends."

I did remember Grier mentioning such a thing in regard to her aging, but I'd not remembered it at all while watching Alasdair cry over my body.

Taking a shaky breath, I relaxed just a little. "Do ye mean it?"

He nodded. "Aye, but that doesna explain the vision. I must cast deeper into yer future, and such spells are not easy. Go back to the village. I'll find ye when I know the truth of what ye saw."

Although relieved that I wasn't near death, my heart was still broken as I walked back to the village.

My brother was days away from losing the love of his life.

Chapter 42

When Hamish stepped into my tent late that evening, he was trembling with exhaustion. I hurried to grab his arms to usher him to a seat.

"What happened? Ye doona look well."

He half-heartedly smiled and motioned to the basin of water across from him.

"Such spells drain strength, most especially when there is much to see." He paused and drank the water I fetched for him. "I have never looked into a future so strange. Ye will not like what I found."

For half of the night, I sat and listened to his strange story, only half believing it but knowing I had no reason to doubt its truth.

"Elspeth will die, lass, there is no way around it, and there is nothing either of us can do to stop it. But yer death is a ruse to save yer brother from a violent clash with Henry's clan."

So Henry would keep his word and spread the news of my witchcraft, and my death is all that could prevent the bloodshed of others. I would gladly fake my death for such a cause.

"Has Henry already threatened action?"

Wearily, Hamish shook his head.

269

"Not yet, but by the time we arrive, yer brother will have received word of the rumors about ye. His own people willna turn, but there are clans around him that will only allow Henry's claims to be ignored once they believe ye dead."

I stood, no longer worried about leaving Jerry. I couldn't help him here anyway. The spell was something only someone far more practiced in magic than I could break. Even then, Hamish's uncle didn't know if he would be successful. My clan was my priority, and it would be until I knew they were safe.

"We should leave in the morning so we have time to arrange everything with Alasdair."

He nodded. "Aye, we shall. Ye do know what this means though, aye?"

Until he asked the question, I'd not stopped to think about the ramifications of faking my own death. I would never be able to see all those I loved. For them, it would seem as if I truly were dead. It would be my last time to see my home, my nephew, my brother.

"Is there not some way for them to know of the ruse? For me to return home once things have settled?"

His gaze was apologetic.

"Yer brother is the only one who may know the truth. And ye willna return home again, at least not for a verra long time. There is more that I saw that I must tell ye."

The reality of how painful such a loss would be for me slowly sunk in. It would tear me in two to leave everyone I knew and loved. But if it kept them safe, I would gladly do it.

"What else?"

He shifted in his seat and rested his arms on his legs. "Grier tricked ye, lass."

"O'course she did. Had I known she would spell him, I would have kept Jerry from her."

"No, 'tis not what I mean. I've said nothing to ye until now because I wanted to be certain I was correct, but my spell this night confirmed it. Ye could have searched for years and never found a spell that would see Jerry home to his own time. There is no spell for such travel. The power to move through time lies with ye and ye alone."

"No." I was insistent in my denial. I knew it couldn't be true. "Grier possesses such a gift, not I. 'Twas she who pulled Jerry from his time and placed him in ours."

"Aye, she too can move others through time but only because she stole part of yer gift from ye. That is what she did to ye that day. She looked inside yer mind for yer talent and took part of it for herself."

I remembered so little from that day, but Alasdair's description came to mind.

"Alasdair said it looked as if power poured from me, as if she were pulling something from inside me."

Hamish nodded. "Aye, she was and 'twas an egregious crime for her to do so. 'Tis why the gift has not presented itself to ye before now—she weakened it. With time, I can help ye restore it."

"I thought our skills were meant to be tied to our destiny. What destiny would require me to move through time?"

Jerry was the obvious choice, but I'd learned enough from Hamish to know that magic wasn't so self-serving. My destiny would lie in aiding others.

"Every person with magic holds two responsibilities. The first is to care and protect their kin and those they love. The

271

second is unique to their ability. That destiny has spoken to you through whispers your entire life. Think, lass, what has always come easily to you? What brings you more joy than just about anything?"

I sat with my memories for a long moment. Over and over again, I noticed a pattern. I could see inside others' hearts and match them with their mate with perfect ease. Countless villagers, Mary and Kip, Mae and Hew, even Alasdair and Elspeth wouldn't have met had it not been for my insistence. While I'd not always possessed such discernment in matters of my own heart, I was skilled at bringing others together.

"Does it have to do with love?"

Smiling, Hamish answered me. "Aye. I told ye I saw verra strange things. It seems the men in yer family are destined to prefer lassies of another century, and yer gift shall bring them together."

"And what of helping my family? Will my death be enough?"

Standing, Hamish walked to the tent's opening.

"For a time, but in several decades another evil shall threaten yer family. We shall see that all is prepared for such a time when we arrive at yer home. I'll explain everything to ye on the way tomorrow. For now, I am weary and need to rest."

I walked to the edge of the tent to see Hamish off. Just as expected, Jerry stood not too far away watching outside his own tent. It was the same every night. I would wave to him, and he would turn his back to me.

I was in no mood to be ignored. Stomping over toward him, I poked him hard in the chest.

"No one is going to be able to break this spell on ye if ye are so intent on remaining miserable. Fight for yerself, Jerry. Fight to be happy."

His jaw tight, Jerry turned away.

"I was happy with Grier, lass. Even if the spell is lifted, I shall never forgive ye for keeping me hostage. I could never love someone so damned foolish."

Chapter 43

T he next morning, Hamish and I packed our horses and prepared to ride to Conall Castle. My heart was heavy for so many reasons, and Hamish simply couldn't stand it.

"He dinna mean it, lass. The spell is fading with time, and 'tis tearing his mind apart as it does. It canna be a pleasant thing—to feel something so strongly only to have everyone around ye telling ye that ye doona really feel the way ye do. I would resist it, as well."

"It pained me as if he meant it."

Hamish finished situating his belongings and came over to grab my hands.

"I know. 'Tis he that is the damned fool. Come with me."

Holding tightly onto my right hand, Hamish led me to Jerry's tent, pushing our way inside without a word. Jerry sat in a chair twiddling away at a piece of wood. His face showed no emotion as he looked at us.

"Stand up, lad."

Jerry didn't move. Hamish repeated himself. "Stand up or I'll pull ye from that chair and knock yer teeth in."

The corner of Jerry's mouth twitched, and I knew he wasn't frightened. He stood anyway.

"What do ye want? I thought the two of ye were leaving this morning. Ye should go. Give my best to everyone at Conall Castle."

He meant the last part. I could tell by the way his features softened. He might be angry with me, but he was still capable of caring for others.

"My uncle has been too gentle with ye. He believes time and patience will be enough to break this spell. I say to hell with it."

Releasing my hand, Hamish walked over to Jerry and grabbed the front of his linen shirt.

"Have ye not noticed how yer moods have changed, lad? When ye dinna believe ye were spelled, ye were pleasant enough. Now, ye are an arse every moment of every bloody day to everyone. Do ye know why that is?"

Jerry didn't flinch with Hamish standing so close. Calmly, without blinking, he answered him. "Mayhap because I'm being kept as a prisoner."

"Lad, if ye wish to see how prisoners are kept, I'll be happy to show ye. I'd prefer if ye were kept in the dungeons anyway. 'Tis not what upsets ye. Ye are angry because ye know ye canna trust yer feelings, and yer frustrated that ye canna find yer way back to the lass standing over there never giving up on ye."

Jerry's eyes shifted toward me for a quick uncomfortable glance. When he said nothing, Hamish continued.

"If ye need some incentive to fight harder, lad, allow me to give it to ye. I am in love with the lass ye are meant for. While I may not be her first choice, I know I could become her second.

If ye doona pull out of this, I shall marry her, and we will send ye on yer merry way back to a life of false love with Grier."

Jerry's face flushed red, and my heart sped up. It was more emotion than I'd seen him elicit in response to me in weeks.

"She doesna love ye, and Morna wouldna ever marry a man she dinna love."

Releasing his grip on Jerry's shirt, Hamish turned and walked toward me, grabbing my arms and pulling me toward him. He spoke to Jerry, but his eyes were locked with mine.

"Her mind has been filled with nothing other than worry over ye and her family. She doesna know what she feels for me. Allow me to give her reason to see that her heart might be more open to me than she knows."

His lips were on mine before I could move. Unlike the last time Jerry watched on as another man kissed me, I feigned nothing as I surrendered to his touch.

Chapter 44

Conall Castle—Six Weeks Later

I would never be ready to say goodbye to him, but I knew it was time. The spell books were in place, the plaque was painted by Hamish's expert hand, and what I knew of the story to come was ready to be told to my brother.

Hamish and I arrived at the castle on the day of Elspeth's death. While I'd kept my promise to her to be back in two months, her labor had come early, and she passed shortly after the delivery.

The weeks that followed were filled with sadness. Most of my days were spent rocking sweet little Arran and holding a heartbroken Eoin while Alasdair dealt with his grief alone.

If not for Mary, Alasdair would've remained lost in his grief for so much longer. Exactly one month after her death, Mary went to his bedchamber and spent hours inside. I suspect none of us will ever know the words she said to him, but I know her well enough to believe she treated him with the tough love he needed to get up and carry on despite the ache in his heart.

I'd told Alasdair of my plan earlier, but it had been during the deepest depths of his grief, and I knew it wouldn't fully hit him until I brought him down to the spell room.

"Ye canna do this, Morna. I canna raise them on my own. I canna bear to lose ye both."

Elspeth's plea remained a heavy weight inside my mind. She would've been so angry with me for leaving him, but I knew the future where they did not. I truly did have no choice.

"If Henry doesna believe me dead, he will gather support from other clans, and yer life here will be overturned. I'll not have blood shed over me."

"We can hide ye here, Morna. We can make them believe ye are dead. No one will ever have to see ye."

Reaching for his hand, I led him down into my spell room.

"No. Such a secret would never keep, and I willna put ye or yer boys in danger. And ye willna be raising them alone. We both know Mary has been the ruler of this castle for as long as she's worked within its walls. Ye will have her to lean on, and ye will do well."

Alasdair seemed to have an endless flow of tears at the ready. As his breath caught on a sob, I paused in the stairwell and threw my arms around him.

I wouldn't cry in front of him. It wouldn't be fair to place my own heartbreak on him, but I'd never hurt so deeply in my life. Alasdair was my best friend and the only family I had left.

"I doona want to do this without ye, lass. I doona have the strength for it."

I held him as if my life depended on it. If I could've stopped time right then, I would've.

"Ye have more strength than ye know. I know what lies ahead, and ye've been through the worst yer life has planned for ye. Ye will be happy again. I promise ye."

He wept into my shoulder. Loud sobs of heartache came from his chest. He sank onto the steps, and I held him as he cried.

"By the time he is grown, Eoin willna remember the spells ye did in front of him. He willna believe any of this. He'll think me mad."

Hours later, cried out for the time being, Alasdair and I were able to discuss all of the final arrangements surrounding what would appear to be my death.

He stood, staring at my open spell books and the painted portrait of Donal MacChristy's daughter, with wide, disbelieving eyes.

"I know, and I doona care what ye decide to tell him as long as ye force him to wed the lass. It willna be Donal's daughter that he marries. The lass who arrives here is the only one who can save yer family."

"Could ye not simply come back yerself and save us? By then, ye will be in no danger. All of this will be but a distant memory."

Even if I didn't already know the destinies of Eoin and the lass from centuries ahead, I wouldn't have wanted to return. Leaving once was already killing me. I never wanted to do it again.

"No, I'm afraid 'tis destined to happen just this way. Can ye promise me ye will do what I ask ye?"

Alasdair nodded.

"Where will ye go, Morna? What will ye do if the spell over Jerry canna be broken?"

I loved Hamish. He was kind and good, and our shared magic helped us relate to one another in a way I would never relate to anyone else. But, my soul didn't long for him.

"I will return with Hamish to Allen territory where I will learn total mastery of all the magic I possess. Afterwards, we will see. Hamish wants me to marry him. I doona know if I can give up on Jerry."

Alasdair placed his hand on my back to lead me from the spell room. He knew what he had to do, and the moment the illusion of me was buried, he would seal the room.

"If 'tis Jerry ye are meant for, doona ever give up on him. Hamish's love for ye is pure, lass. He wishes for ye to be happy, even if 'tis not with him. Come lass, I've arranged for a portrait to be painted of us all. I must have some way to look at ye after ye are gone. I only wish I'd done the same with Elspeth. We will have one last evening together then I will bid ye farewell."

Tears I promised myself I wouldna cry fell as a desperate need to be near him filled me. I flung my arms around him once more.

"If there was any other way, I would never leave ye. Ye canna begin to know how much I love ye. There has never been a lass alive with a greater brother than mine."

Kissing the top of my hair, Alasdair whispered, "I know exactly how much ye love me for 'tis only a fraction of how much I love ye. Ye may be gone from here, but my love will never leave ye. Ye will feel it inside ye every day of yer life."

And I did. Until Alasdair took his last breath several decades later, he was with me every single day.

Chapter 45

Allen Territory

Jerry was gone when we returned to Allen territory. Hamish's uncle met us at their border with the news.

"He's been gone a fortnight. He escaped in the night. All that was left in his tent was this note."

I took the note and opened it. Inside he'd scribbled the words, "*I've gone to fight for ye. Please doona marry him.*"

Hamish directed his horse nearer mine so he could read the words over my shoulder. "He's gone to Grier, lass. We must go to him."

I turned and looked into Hamish's sad, accepting eyes.

"Would ye have ever stopped trying to break the spell? Why have ye helped me when ye doona truly want him to break it?"

I knew his answer even before he said—Hamish's heart was too good.

"What I told Jerry that day was true. I am in love with ye, and love is selfless. I would have kept trying to break the spell until the day ye were ready to give up on him. I would've waited years had it taken that long. If ever the time had come when ye

285

were ready, I would've gladly cherished ye as my wife. But, I've already lost, lass, and I know it. Let us go and get Jerry—the real Jerry—so ye can find happiness for the first time in far too many months."

MacNeal Territory

Much to my surprise, Grier had remained in Henry's service, feigning work as an herbal healer to hide her magic from him.

She knew we were coming. She met us outside as we approached her home.

"He's not here. The spell is broken."

Gone was the mirage of a young, beautiful woman. She looked to be a hundred years old—frightened, sad, and broken.

"Where's he gone?"

"I thought ye were dead. I felt ye were dead. What sort of magic broke the bond between us?"

I'd done nothing, but I understood her confusion. I'd known she wasn't dead when Alasdair thought she was because I could still feel her magic. Hamish had done something to break our bond.

I looked at him and he nodded in confirmation before speaking. "Ye will no longer break the rules of magic, Grier. If ye steal from another, I will kill ye myself."

"Was that why we were connected? Because she stole from me?"

"Aye."

A sinking feeling settled in my gut as I realized what Jerry's absence must mean.

"Where is he?"

She smiled, and I had to hold tight to my horse's reins to keep from flying off the horse and grabbing her around the throat.

"He thinks ye are dead. I wouldna have broken the spell, otherwise. Even with ye gone, he dinna want me. He's returned to Conall Castle to seek work from yer brother."

I turned my horse around to leave. She wasn't worth another breath, but she screamed a curse at me as we left. "May ye never bear children, and may Jerry's heart be weak. May chaos follow the two of ye always."

I nudged my horse into a run. I never wanted to see her again.

I rode for a long while before I realized I was alone, and I only realized it then because of a galloping horse approaching.

I looked over my shoulder to see Hamish.

"I thought ye were behind me. Where did ye go?"

"To speak to her. I havena ever seen anyone carry such pain."

I could feel no sympathy for her.

"She deserves every bit of pain she feels. What did ye tell her?"

"Only that there was hope for her still, if only she learns to forgive herself first."

I shook my head and gave Hamish a small smile. "'Tis good that Grier's spell is broken. I would have been entirely undeserving of ye. Ye are one of the kindest men I've ever known."

Conall Territory

We were much more careful as we approached Conall Castle. I'd been so sure I would never return to my home that I could scarcely believe I was back only a few days later.

We tied our horses near a stream in a secluded part of the woods. I was to remain hidden while Hamish went to find Alasdair and Jerry.

The wait seemed like days, though I know it must've been only a few hours at most. When I heard footsteps approaching, I kept myself hidden until I heard their voices. I'd expected only Hamish and Jerry, but at the sound of my brother's voice, I pulled away from the brush and ran to him.

He caught me as I jumped toward him, my feet lifting off the ground. He pulled me into a hug as his choked voice spoke into my ear.

"I couldna not see ye again, if ye were here. Besides, Jerry and I have a plan."

I looked over Alasdair's back. Jerry's eyes were filled with tears. "Let go of yer brother, lass. I need ye in my arms this instant."

Alasdair released me, but my steps toward Jerry were much more hesitant.

"Ye told me once ye would never forgive me for keeping ye captive. Is it true?"

He shook his head. "No. There is nothing ye could do that I wouldna forgive. Can ye forgive me for all the things I said to ye? All the pain that I caused?"

Alasdair interrupted before I could answer him. "O'course she will, lad. There will be plenty of time for the two of ye to be alone. For now, we must make haste before either of ye is discovered."

"No one knows Jerry is here?"

Alasdair shook his head. "No. I knew if Mary saw him, 'twould raise too many questions. As soon as he arrived, I told him the truth of what happened. He wished to go after ye, but I knew if I kept him here, I'd get to see ye one last time." Alasdair paused and leaned in to whisper, "Ye should have seen him, lass. The thought that ye were gone...he felt the loss as acutely as I felt Elspeth's."

"Yer brother wishes to marry us."

I listened as the pair of them took turns explaining their plan, and for the first time in months, all was well.

In the middle of the night, with a full moon and a blanket full of stars as our only light, Jerry and I promised to spend the rest of our lives together.

I'm not certain you could say we were ever officially married. Alasdair performed the ceremony and a druid was our only witness, but our vows were no less sacred. Ours was an unusual courtship—it seemed fitting that our wedding be unusual as well.

Once we sealed our promises with a kiss, I bid my brother one last final farewell, and we left Conall Castle for good.

Allen Territory—Three Months Later

"Ach, lass, I willna ever get tired of bedding ye. Thank God, they moved us to a proper cottage. Otherwise, the whole village would be hearing the ruckus we make every night."

I laughed as he collapsed on top of me, his lips trailing gentle, lazy kisses down my neck.

"Even when we are old and gray and our bones creak when we walk?"

"Even then."

Rolling to face him as he slid off me, I smiled in excitement as I readied myself to share my news with him. "I have something to tell ye."

"Oh?" He twisted his head and raised his brow to encourage me to get on with it.

"I've decided ye were right about something ye suggested to me long ago."

"What's that, lass? I've never known myself to be right about anything."

"Do ye remember when I told ye what I saw in the spell I cast? The home from yer time, with the lass inside it?"

He nodded but said nothing.

"I think mayhap she was me. Are ye ready to go home?"

The one thing I'd once promised myself I would never do—leave this time, my home, and my family—was now my greatest wish. I couldn't return home anyway. It was time for Jerry and me to start a life of our own—a fresh start in a fresh time.

"Are ye saying ye've learned to do it? To travel through time?"

"Aye, I have."

Jerry reached to pull me against him, devouring me with a kiss that left my head free of all thought. When he pulled away, he looked down over his nose at me.

"When can we leave?"

"In the morning, if ye wish it."

"Oh, I wish it, lass. Now, let me bed ye here one last time for memories sake."

I woke early to sneak away while Jerry still slept. There was one last thing I needed to tend to, one last goodbye I had to make.

Hamish was awake when I slipped into his tent. He sat on the edge of his bed, already dressed in his kilt, as if he were waiting for me.

"Ye are leaving then, aye?"

I went over to join him and grabbed his hands as I sat down on the bed.

"Aye. I've something I wish to give ye."

"Ye owe me nothing."

I smiled and reached up to place one hand on his cheek.

"I owe ye more than ye will ever know. I doona wish to repay ye. I wish to give ye the gift of hope."

Reaching into the bosom of my dress, I pulled out a folded piece of parchment and extended it in his direction. Smiling, I released my grip on his other hand.

"Open it."

I watched and waited as he looked down at his own piece of art. When he looked up at me, his brows were furrowed.

"This looks like my hand."

"'Tis yer hand." I paused and pointed to the various faces in the portrait. "And that there is ye, although I'll admit ye've allowed yerself to age by the time ye draw this. And there is yer wife, and yer daughter and her husband, and do ye see the wee lad on yer lap? That is little Raudrich. 'Tis yer grandson."

Hamish's eyes slowly filled with tears.

"Where did ye get this?"

"It took me most of the day yesterday to land precisely where I wished to, but I traveled to yer future to give ye hope in the now. I know ye love me, Hamish, and I love ye more than I hope Jerry ever knows, but ye yerself said I was meant for another. The love of yer life is meant only for ye. As ye can see, ye do find her."

Hamish and I visited until dawn then parted ways as the dearest of friends.

The entire village of Allen territory came to see us off. As Jerry and I disappeared into the future, I knew our adventure together was only beginning.

Note from M.C.:

Well, there you have it. I told you everything would turn out well in the end, even if there were some heartaches and times of sadness along the way.

Now that you're finished, I've no doubt you must think me completely mad. But isn't there some tiny part of you that wonders if all of this could be true?

If you wish to find out, you'll have to come and see for yourself.

We now live in that little inn I saw in my first vision of Jerry's future. While it is not visible to most, you should have no trouble finding it. Just follow the road leading to Conall Castle. We are on the right, no more than a few miles from the castle gates.

See you soon. I'll have Jerry put the kettle on straight away.

Epilogue

Present Day

L aurel closed the book and looked up for the first time all day.

"Marcus, do you remember passing an inn on the way back from Conall Castle?"

"If I remember correctly, we passed at least two dozen inns. We're a good two hours from Conall Castle. Not that you would know with the way your head has been buried in that book all day. Was it really that good?"

Laurel knew that Marcus would think her request absurd, but there was no way she was waiting until morning.

"Would you like to see Scotland by dark?"

"Do you want to go to a pub?"

Smiling, she reached for his hand and tried to pull him out of his seat.

"No. I'll drive this time. I know just where we're going."

Marcus handed Laurel the keys and followed behind her. "And where is that?"

"To the inn near Conall Castle."

"Now, that stretch I do remember. There was nothing in the thirty miles leading to the castle."

"There will be now, and I don't want to be late for tea."

Morna's Legacy will continue. Visit Bethany's website and sign up for her mailing list to be notified about new releases.

About The Author

Bethany Claire is the USA Today Bestselling Author of the Scottish time travel romance novels in Morna's Legacy Series.

Bethany's love of storytelling has been a lifelong passion but, convinced it would serve her best to follow a "conventional" career path, she tucked that passion away and went off to college.

Fast forward four years and about six major changes later, she realized the stories simply were not going to stay tucked away. Months away from graduating with a degree in elementary education, she finally realized writing was the only career that would make her happy.

So one day in the middle of a summer education course, she got up in the middle of class and walked to the registrar's office and withdrew from the university on the spot. Since then, she has devoted herself to writing full time and is following her dreams.

Read more about Bethany at www.bethanyclaire.com..

Connect With Me Online

http://www.bethanyclaire.com
http://twitter.com/BClaireAuthor
http://facebook.com/bethanyclaire
http://www.pinterest.com/bclaireauthor

If you enjoyed reading *Love Beyond Reach,* I would appreciate it if you would help others enjoy this book, too.

Recommend it. Help other readers find this book by recommending it to friends, readers' groups and discussion boards.

Review it. Please tell other readers why you like this book by reviewing it at the retailer of your choice. If you do write a review, please send me an email to bclaire@bethanyclaire.com so I can thank you with a personal email, or you can visit my website at http://www.bethanyclaire.com

Join the Bethany Claire Newsletter!

Sign up for my newsletter to receive up-to-date information of books, new releases, events, and promotions.

http://bethanyclaire.com/contact.php#mailing-list

Acknowledgements

This book has been a work in progress for a very long time and wouldn't be finished today without the help and patience of some really wonderful and generous people.

Mom, thank you for all of the long hours and for remaining patient even when I know you're ready to pull my hair out. I know the tight deadlines drive you crazy. I so appreciate you putting up with my creative nature anyway.

Karen, Elizabeth, Marsha, Johnetta, & Vivian, you ladies are appreciated more than you know. Your keen eyes and suggestions play a vital role in getting these books ready. I'm so appreciative of your patience. I know the way I go about things is often a challenge.

Dj, as always, thanks for fitting me in and dealing with things in chunks.

To every Morna's Legacy reader, thank you for patiently waiting for Morna's story. I know you've been waiting on it for a very long time. And for all of you who have asked – this is not the last book – Morna's Legacy will continue…

Made in the USA
San Bernardino, CA
10 May 2018